Praise for Davi

"Peak knows his metal, and a insight into the frontiers of fringe culture. Max, Roland, and Seph are sadly believable, despite their world being profoundly darker than even they had morbidly dreamed. No punches are pulled. No killer riff left unplayed. *Corpsepaint* pushed all three of my buttons: Extreme Metal, Lovecraftian Horror, and GOATS!"

—Nathan Carson, author of *Starr Creek*,
drummer of Witch Mountain

"*Corpsepaint* is an imaginative, doom-laden foray into the contested domain coupling black metal's disabused hostility to liberal-capitalist ideology with an ethereal and perforce transgressive henosis of hate."

—Edia Connole, co-author of *Floating Tomb: Black Metal Theory*

"Novels about rock bands are usually just that: novels about rock bands: depictions, imitations. Peak's *Corpsepaint* is much more than that. It captures the dark spirit, howling aesthetic and nihilistic philosophy of black metal and makes it the motor of the fiction. A grim and unforgiving book that steps deeply into the darkness and invites you to follow."

—Brian Evenson, author of *A Collapse of Horses*

"Beautifully, wonderfully, tragically dismal! Thought provoking horror that reaches deep inside you, rips out your still-beating heart, then asks you to consider what it means."

—Amber Fallon, author of *The Warblers*

"A work of true cosmic horror set in the death-tinged world of the black metal scene. Peak drags the reader below ground to confront forces seeking to spread a powerful, ancient darkness. *Corpsepaint* is a bleak, terrifying ride."

—Michael Griffin, author of *The Human Alchemy*

Other Books by David Peak

Surface Tension

The River Through the Trees

The Spectacle of the Void

Eyes in the Dust

DAVID PEAK

WORD HORDE
PETALUMA, CA

For Max Ulve—this one is ours

Without music life would be a mistake.

—Nietzsche

PART ONE
HENOSIS

1

CHICAGO, 3 AM

Roland woke beneath a heavy weight, a shadow in the dark room. He opened his eyes and saw a black motorcycle boot planted mere inches from his skull.

The image that took form in his mind, rising up out of the mucky swirl of sleep, was that old painting, Fuseli's *Nightmare*, or some version of it, the one with the woman in the white dress lying on her back, that furry devil-thing sitting on her chest. The look on that devil-thing's face, it looked like—

"Max?" Roland said, or tried to say, his voice scraping up and out his throat. Still half asleep, disoriented, it took him a few seconds to realize that Max had one hand around his neck, thumb and first finger clamped down.

This is real, Roland thought, strangely calm, resigned to whatever it was that was happening. Here he was, getting murdered.

Through the windows at the end of the room, the sodium streetlights glowed orange, casting dim light at play in syrupy pools of darkness—the early morning hours. Winter winds pressed cruelly against the glass, snowflakes caustic, as blinding as TV static. Max's grip on Roland's throat loosened slightly. He struggled with his back pocket with his free hand.

"What the fuck, dude," Roland said, voice pinched and phlegmy. He tried to move but was trapped inside his sleeping bag, bound. He vaguely remembered passing out here after untold hours of drinking and smoking, staying up late, playing records, taking a few unmarked pills someone had given him, rolling out his sleeping bag on the floor of Max's living room, sometime early in the morning, he guessed. Max must have stayed up all night, kept drinking long after everyone else had left or blacked out. Fuck, was Max blacked out? Earlier that night, Roland had heard dozens of stories about this, about Max blacking out, had been warned that he became violent, unpredictable. All this from people who knew him well, or seemed to at least: former bandmates, long-time friends, an ex with murder in her eyes, all people who had been putting up with him for nearly two decades.

A long strand of dirty blond hair fell from behind Max's ear as he brought his free hand forward, a broken and worn sunglasses case squeezed tight in his red fist. Roland knew that this was where Max kept his works, had seen it come out once or twice the night before. "You're a poser," Max said, his voice gnarled from too many cigarettes, not enough sleep, spitting out the insult like a poison, as if it were the absolute worst thing he could say about another person. "All you next-generation posers are pussies. You write songs about death and dying and you don't know what it feels like to be dead. You don't know shit."

Max let go of Roland's throat and slid to the floor, one leg still extended over Roland's chest. He quietly sang the opening lyrics to the Beatles' "She Said She Said," voice angelic. He was out of his mind. Max unzipped the case and dumped out its contents. Roland quickly got one arm out of his sleeping bag, pulled the zipper down until it snagged on the cloth, and struggled out from beneath Max's heavy leg. Fuck, he never would have even guessed that Max would listen to the Beatles.

His head was pounding, though it was difficult to tell if it was from fear or the lingering effects of the booze, the first inklings of a killer hangover. The pills he had taken earlier, he couldn't tell what they were doing to him, if they were doing anything to him at all.

"Fucking asshole," he said, rubbing his throat. "What is your problem?" Max looked up and their eyes met and then Roland realized how far gone Max really was. He felt a flush of heated panic bloom in his chest. Max's eyelids looked inflamed, nearly swollen shut, and his mouth hung open, lower lip glistening with spit. He was forty-two, twenty years older than Roland, but he looked really old, like fifty. Max snapped a needle into place on the syringe, then picked up a small plastic baggie with two long, tattooed fingers; a thin trace of powder lined its bottom.

"Shit," Max said. "Somebody must have done all my shit. Do you know who did all my shit?" Roland knew for a fact that Max never let his works out of his sight, that he'd most likely shot up or snorted or smoked whatever he had left, but still he said nothing, just shook his head. Max quickly stuffed everything back into the sunglasses case, zipped it up, and stumbled to his feet, nearly colliding with the couch, an arm against the wall for balance.

The whole apartment smelled like whiskey.

Roland took it all in, the smell. He could breathe again, his heart pumping in his throat. It made him feel sick, like he was choking on it. He'd never really believed that Max could be dangerous, despite all of the stories. Even for a black-metal band, Angelus Mortis had a reputation for controversy that was legendary: in ten years Max, who wrote and performed under the *nom de guerre* Strigoi, had burned through nearly thirty hired guns; he'd gotten himself banned from a festival in

Florida after it had been discovered that a white supremacist label distributed some of his CD-Rs; been dropped from a well-respected label after he'd failed to deliver an album on time; and most recently, alienated his most ardent fans after he'd pocketed the cash from merch sales online and never delivered the goods.

He was a bad dude, by all accounts, but his music was good—no one could deny that. It was sometimes even great, especially his early albums, which were now considered classics, the albums that had successfully introduced the American black-metal scene to the rest of the world, established it as something the European snobs could take seriously. And his gigs paid good money. Real money, too, not drink tickets.

Just in case Roland really doubted that Strigoi's reputation as a psychopath was warranted, Max took a few long strides across the room, alarmingly quick, and swung his boot, connected solidly with Roland's thigh. The pain was instant, bone deep. Roland cried out, more surprised than hurt, though it certainly did hurt.

"Get up, pussy," Max said, looming over Roland, wavering slightly. "Let's go."

What choice did Roland have? He'd just arrived in Chicago from Seattle the previous morning, all of his worldly possessions packed into a single duffel bag, and the next day—*to-day*—they were flying to Prague, an all-expenses-paid trip to meet up with the infamous members of Wisdom of Silenus in Ukraine and record an album on their compound, an almost unheard-of honor and once-in-a-lifetime opportunity. He was at Max's mercy. He had no other friends in the city, no one he could call—didn't even have enough money to get back home if he wanted to. And besides, it's not like he had anywhere to go there, either. In fact, there were more than a few people back home he'd rather avoid entirely.

"It's freezing outside," Roland said, his voice weak, sounding every bit like a pussy. Max had him pegged. He didn't know what he'd gotten himself into. When people asked him why he'd accepted an offer to write material and play drums on Max's latest album, the supposed comeback album, he'd told them the truth: he liked being employed. The money that Max offered wasn't bad either. And the free trip to Europe and Ukraine had sealed the deal.

"Put on a fucking jacket," Max said.

A few minutes later they were down on the street, waiting for a bus, Roland shivering in his boots, hoodie up, hands stuffed in the pockets of his thin denim jacket. Although he was having a hard time walking a straight line, Max seemed to have sobered up a bit.

The night was so cold Roland's bones ached. The city was dead quiet, blanketed with pristine snow, the headlights of the bus barely visible through the downfall as it appeared in the distance. Roland fed a few dollar bills into the fare machine. Neither of them said a word for the entire bus ride. The interior of the bus was filled with harsh light. Max almost nodded off a few times, dropped his phone on the floor at one point and cracked the screen, hair hanging down in front of his face. And then they were getting off somewhere on the near south side, just outside Chinatown. They walked a few blocks, still not talking, and stood below the archaic elevated tracks. Max turned and jabbed Roland in the chest with a single finger. "Wait here," he said. "I'm gonna pick up some rock." A train roared by overhead, impossibly loud, as Max stumbled off into the night. In the distance, maybe two blocks away, Roland could just barely make out two red-brick buildings surrounded by chain-link fence that looked like the projects.

A woman's voice interrupted Roland's thoughts: "You got

any change?" She was older, middle-aged, stepped into the blustery light of the streetlamp as if appearing out of nowhere. Her parka was covered with filth, the once-white faux-fur lining the hood now the color of rotting teeth.

"Fuck off," Roland said. "What do I look like?" He kicked at her, not seriously, just to shoo her away. "Get the fuck out of here." The woman stormed off, muttering, never even looked Roland in the eyes. He'd only been in Chicago for, what, two days? And already he found it a miserable place. How could anyone live here? Or why would they, considering the cold. Where did the homeless sleep at night during the winter? He'd heard stories before of people freezing to death at night in places like this, drunks stumbling home after a night at the bar who fell on the ice and hit their heads, or maybe they got home, couldn't find their keys, and lay down to wait for morning, only morning never arrived—just permanent night. Not the worst way to go, by any means. Painless. Exactly something a pussy would think, opting for a painless death. Fuck. Max had been gone now for what, ten, fifteen minutes? What if he was passed out somewhere, in an alley somewhere, behind a dumpster somewhere, freezing to death? Fuck him. But then how would he explain to the cops that he'd let his friend—his *acquaintance*, really—walk away to die? Would he even have to talk to the police? Of course he would. He couldn't live with something like that on his conscience. Because he was a pussy. He'd have to tell them that he hadn't even searched for him. I mean, Max wasn't even really his friend. More of a colleague. An employer.

Roland quickly walked to the end of the block and looked in all four directions. Nothing. Snow everywhere. No sign of Max. No sign of anyone—just the two red-brick buildings down the street. No choice.

"God dammit," he muttered.

Stomach in knots and now, weirdly enough, overwhelmed by a sudden hunger, an acidic pit burning a hole in his guts, Roland made his way over to the projects. The building was four stories, drab, surrounded by a chain-link fence; a few of the units still had their lights on. Roland followed the sidewalk, crunching huge chunks of scattered salt with his boots, as it curved and led to a shitty little courtyard between the two buildings. A motion-sensor lamp clicked on, filling the courtyard with harsh, yellow light.

Roland froze. Ten seconds of silence passed. A deep voice boomed from one of the units above: "Motherfucker looks lost."

And then nothing—just more silence. Roland felt the creepiness of knowing you're being watched, not knowing who's doing the watching or from where—it was the kind of thing that made his skin crawl. He looked one way, the cramped lobby of the building visible through the metal door's small, reinforced-glass window. Nothing. Then the other way: the same sight, only this time there were the unmistakable prints of Max's motorcycle boots in the snow leading to the door. Instantly regretting his decision, but unable to help himself, Roland held up both middle fingers, raised his arms up to the units above, and turned in a tight circle. He was angry now, angry because he was scared, though he'd never admit it to himself.

"The fuck outta here, bitch," the voice called back.

The intercom was busted open, scorched black, a snake's nest of multicolored wires blooming beneath the panel, and the door was left cracked open. Roland leaned into the door and felt it thump into something in the lobby, heard a grunt, the distinct sound of a body slumping over. He slid inside. Yellow light was everywhere, nearly blinding—the thick stench of stale cigarette smoke. Max lay on his side against the wall, one arm splayed out to the side, his palm slicked with bright red blood. One of his fingers twitched slightly. A matching streak of blood stained the tiled wall, curved downward, illustrating the trajectory of Max's fall.

"Fuck," Roland said, kneeling down. "Max? Can you hear me?" He unzipped Max's leather jacket. His T-shirt was dry—no visible stab wounds to the abdomen at least. Max lightly patted the back of his head, sucking air through his clenched teeth, his hand coming away freshly slicked with blood. "Let me see the back of your head," Roland said, batting away Max's listless attempt to stop him. "Move your hand, dude—I need to see how bad it is." There was blood everywhere. Roland carefully parted a few long strands of Max's hair, revealing countless tiny shards of glittering brown glass, but no source of the bleeding. "They burned me," Max said. "Kids. One of 'em came up behind me and swung a bottle at my head. Took my money and ran." Roland ignored him, parted another section of Max's hair, revealing a thin, crooked gash just over his right ear. He'd seen much worse. "It's not a bad cut," he said, "just bleeding a lot."

The sound of clipped, concerned conversation echoed down the stairwell at the end of the lobby, a woman and a few men.

"Come on," Roland said, threading an arm under Max's shoulder.

Max groaned. It took him nearly thirty seconds to find the strength in his legs. "I need to get my seven bucks back." He slurred his speech, tried to pull Roland toward the stairs. Roland didn't even argue. He pivoted and muscled Max along with him toward the door.

The voices from the stairwell were getting louder, coming closer, closing in. Roland pushed open the door with his free hand. Already he was sweating beneath his jacket, his face flushed with heat. The light in the courtyard was still on. He heard a police siren in the distance. Already? But how? "Come on," Roland said. "You need to use your fucking legs. Bend your knees, asshole." Looking back at how far they'd come, Roland saw a trail of wine-dark droplets of blood in the snow.

Max's whole body shuddered. The hand he'd been using to put pressure on the bleeding fell slack at his side and the sudden shift in weight threw Roland off balance. The two of them toppled into the snow, Max first, Roland landing weirdly on the arm still wrapped beneath Max's shoulder.

For a few still moments, Roland actually heard Max softly snoring, as if his body and mind were both intent on shutting down at the worst possible moment. "Jesus Christ," Roland said. "Wake the fuck up." He managed to get his arm free from beneath Max's torso, raised his hand up high—the memory of Max kicking his thigh flashed in his mind, all of the fear, the confusion of the night building into a blinding white light, a white-hot rage—and slapped Max's open mouth as hard as he could. The sound echoed throughout the courtyard, as loud as cracking ice.

One of Max's eyes fluttered open, the other stubbornly swollen shut. Max drooled a bit, his one open eye focusing on Roland. His bottom lip was split, a glistening dab of dark blood at its center. "Need to get my seven bucks back," he said.

"I'll fucking give you seven bucks if you stand up and walk back to the train with me," Roland said. Max seemed to nod slightly. A few moments later, Roland was on his feet, helping Max up out of the snow. They quickly left the courtyard behind, turning out into the street just as a police cruiser flew by, lights blaring, way over the speed limit. Another car, this one unmarked, lights on the dash, quickly followed. Wherever they were going, whatever was happening, it was more important than what was happening here. Roland released the breath he hadn't known he'd been holding all this time, breathed in deep, and felt suddenly lightheaded as the oxygen hit his brain.

They walked for what felt like an hour, Max slowly gaining control of his faculties, leading the way. Eventually they came across people crowding the sidewalk outside a standalone three-flat on a deserted industrial street, the last lingering dregs of the 4 AM bar scene. The sidewalk was flooded with red light. Everyone was drunk, smoking, being obnoxious; no one seemed to notice the stains of dried blood on Max's face. "I know people here," Max said. "Wait here." He quickly ducked in through the front door, leaving Roland on the sidewalk.

Roland's hands were totally numb. He looked at them. The black scabs on his knuckles had peeled, giving way to the shiny, tender pink skin beneath. He ran a thumb over the new skin and licked his chapped lips. He wanted nothing more than to be back in his sleeping bag on Max's living room floor, to take a fiery swig of whiskey and feel the slow warmth spread through his chest. Their flight to Prague was leaving in fourteen hours, plenty of time for Max to clean himself up and get his shit together, for Roland to crash and recharge. There was no backing out now, even if Max was crazy or violent or whatever. There was nothing to worry about, really. The old fucker probably wouldn't even remember any of this. Soon enough they'd be focusing on the music. That's what this trip was all about. There would be many strange things. And even though Roland knew something of what strange things there would be, he was still impossibly excited about whatever it was that existed beyond the limits of his imagination.

This is what Roland focused on, whatever was beyond

expectations, as they piled into the back of a cramped sedan that belonged to one of Max's friends from the bar, as they climbed the narrow and steep steps to Max's apartment, exhausted. Max crashed face first onto the couch, still wearing his boots and jacket. Roland zipped himself up in his shitty sleeping bag once again, fought the urge to cry, because he wasn't a pussy and he certainly wasn't scared. This was the life he had always wanted. This was what he'd always wanted, deep down inside. He knew it was true. So what the fuck was he crying about?

2

Roland worried that the TSA wouldn't let Max through the security gate. With his hoodie pulled up, and his face hidden behind mirror shades, he was a dead ringer for the Unabomber. It certainly didn't help that the two of them together smelled like a bar at last call.

Max handed over his passport and his boarding pass. His chipped nail polish and webby, blown-out tattoos made his hand look gangrenous in the harsh light of the terminal. The TSA agent, a heavyset guy with a short, dark beard and sharp eyes, instructed Max to lose the glasses.

Fuck, Roland thought, here we go.

Max's eyes were bloodshot, glassy. A trickle of dried blood curled down his neck from behind his ear. In all likelihood, he was probably still fucked up from the night before, a good enough reason alone not to let him through. But the TSA agent smirked, cocked an eyebrow, and gave Max a knowing look—a been-there-before kind of look—and ushered him through.

Max put a hand on Roland's shoulder and said, "You were a real bro last night. I won't forget that." He paused for a second. And then, "We're gonna get this album done and it's gonna exist because of you. I'll make sure people know that." And just like that, Roland felt his lingering resentment toward Max, all the hatred and fear and anger from the night before, begin to slip away. It was something in the way Max spoke to him, something in the way he let his hand rest so casually on Roland's shoulder, like he really trusted him, like it was a totally normal thing to do. Even if he was being manipulated, and he had a very strong inclination that this was the case, Roland didn't care. Max needed him to make an album and people, the press, all of those fans, they cared about the albums that Max made. People wrote about the albums that Max made. Magazines wrote features that ranked all of the Angelus Mortis albums; editors included the early albums on lists of essential black-metal albums. They were going to make something that could survive the ages.

By the time they got to the gate, the plane was nearly finished boarding. Max got on first, stomped all the way to the back row, and took the window seat without even so much as a second thought, selfish bastard. By the time Roland buckled his seat belt, Max was slumped up against the window, out cold. Roland took out the only book he'd brought with him, the only book he even owned anymore, a tattered old paperback that traced the influence of the occult through art history. He wasn't big on the essays up front, they were almost impossible to understand, but the rest of the book consisted of hundreds of detailed, full-color photos, beginning with the Renaissance, the Baroque period, and then moving on through Gothic art, even Modernism, which was mostly bullshit. Considering the way Roland had lived the last few years of his life, it was a miracle he'd held on to the thing. And yet here he held it in his hands, an atlas of his adult life. He flipped to one of his favorites, Friedrich's *Wanderer above the Sea of Fog*, and hungrily studied the texture of the clouds. A few moments later and they were in the air, bound for their layover in Warsaw.

Looking over Max's shoulder, Roland watched the gray-slab skyline of Chicago through the tiny window as it shrank down and disappeared beneath the blustery winter weather. He was relieved to be leaving it behind, and not just because it was a cold and dead place. No, he was relieved to leave behind a version of himself that hadn't really lived, because now he would really start living the life he was meant to live. This was the first time he'd left the country. Just two days ago, Roland had never really left the Pacific Northwest, never traveled farther than a couple of tour stops in Vancouver or Portland, and now here he was, up in the air, cruising over the world below, a wanderer in his own right.

Roland drank four vodka tonics in the next two hours and slipped into a fitful, grudging sleep. The rest of the flight blurred together, didn't feel all that much different from a long and uncomfortable ride in a tour van, except there was even less to look at, no gas-station pit stops and shitty beer and Zeppelin on the radio. Max woke up once or twice, gestured wordlessly that he had to get up, and stumbled to the bathrooms. Traveling really wasn't all it was cracked up to be, Roland thought. And yet people talked about it like they talked about where they went to college, like it was all that they were, an indication of self-worth. Because deep down inside, everyone hated themselves. That's how people were. Pathetic. They sniffed out ways to figure out how you'd grown up, asked what your parents did, where you went to school. No one gave two shits about Roland as soon as they found out he'd dropped out in the tenth grade, or that he'd grown up in the white-trash sticks of the Pacific Northwest, running away from home and joining a death metal band in Bellingham and then getting hooked on smack like all the other poor and pathetic Seattle street kids. And he didn't give two shits about any of them, either. Fuck them. All that resentment, he took it out on his drums. The bullshit was just fuel for his craft.

But that was all a long time ago—a lifetime ago. He'd put all of that behind him and he was clean now and he was flying to Europe with the one and only Strigoi to write an album and soon they—all of those snobby fuckers—would be writing magazine articles about him.

They had just enough time at the airport in Warsaw to eat at a McDonald's, which seemed to attract only other tourists, and drink a beer or two at some shitty little bar, soccer games on mute on the half-dozen TVs. One more quick flight after that and they touched down in the Czech Republic, where Roland had no idea if the people even spoke English or what kind of food they ate or what kind of money they used.

In the cab ride to Pankrác, a working-class neighborhood where the record label had booked them a few nights at a pension, Max sat slumped in his seat, boots splayed wide, and ashed his cigarette through the crack in the window. He was manic, talking Roland's ear off. He talked about how in the twenty years he'd been doing this—making music, recording albums, and touring—he'd never before had an advance big enough to do anything other than pay a few months' rent, cover a handful of bar tabs. And yet here they were, in motherfucking Eastern Europe, where they'd been given a decent per diem, a few long days to see the sights.

The pension was a boring scene, nothing more than a narrow four-story building filled with American kids on their first European tour, a few Macedonians who kept to themselves, a shifty-eyed Russian dude who sat drinking cup after cup after cup of sludgy coffee in the lounge, chain-smoking Gauloises. They dropped off their bags in their room and headed straight back out, didn't even bother changing their clothes, found the first pub down the street—there were pubs everywhere—and started drinking, shots of Russian Standard followed by pints of Budweiser Budvar, which was nothing like the Budweiser back in the States. They paid in dollars, just threw a wad of bills up on the bar where it got snatched up without comment. Everything was dirt cheap. For the first time in his life, Roland got a sense of the limitlessness of money, of the freedom it afforded. He felt drunk almost immediately, a surge of raw power flowing through his veins. They took two more shots of Russian Standard. The beer was so cheap it was basically free— but it was also good, crisp, maybe even the best he'd ever had.

Then they were back out on the street, on their way to the next place, following the Vltava River up into Prague 2. Max, it seemed, knew his way around quite well, and so Roland simply followed, allowing the whole evening to open up before him like a cheap whore.

On the street level, Prague looked old world, all winding streets, cobblestones, and gothic architecture, like something out of an old black-and-white horror movie, creeping shadows and lamplight, church steeples and stone gargoyles. In the distance, glass-and-steel high-rises towered above the surrounding rooftops, monolithic intrusions of the modern world. That was just the way things were. The world had a way of never letting you forget it was there, still surrounding you, reminding you that there was no escaping how crushingly boring it really was. Magic, whatever you wanted to call it, the illusion of things, always evaporated under scrutiny. There was a light dusting of snow over everything, gleaming in the moonlight, but compared to the brutal chill of Chicago, the cold here was nothing. The streets were filled with people. Roland heard half a dozen languages in the span of a hundred yards. A large group of English soccer hooligans, arm in arm, chanting something unintelligible, wearing identical red jerseys, all shaved heads and bulky shoulders, plowed through the crowd.

Max and Roland ate at a KFC of all places because they were already half drunk, neither of them were adventurous eaters, and it was something familiar. They ate greasy pieces of fried chicken out of greasy paper buckets, standing at a little counter, watching the people walk by the restaurant's front window. Max smacked his lips as he ate, wiped his mouth with the sleeve of the flannel he wore under his jacket, clamped down on the bones and bared his teeth, laughing like a wild kid. And then they were back in the street, up in what appeared to be a ritzy business area, the streets widening, the surrounding buildings more imposing, governmental. They walked for what felt like no time at all and, despite this, Roland felt himself sobering up, remembered the endless trudge through the icy streets of Chicago, following after a bloodied and stewing Max, only now things were so much different. His heart felt light in his chest. Now he was following a legendary rock god in a foreign city that was so magical it might as well have been Disney World. They entered a large square. A medieval castle loomed majestic in the distance, its two impressive towers lit with purple lights. They stopped in at another pub. Another round of shots and Budweiser—shit was magic. And then back into the street. Max constantly ten feet ahead of Roland, telling him to hurry the fuck up. The fried chicken wasn't sitting well with Roland. Too much travel, maybe. Come to think of it, he'd felt like shit ever since they'd landed, just hadn't taken the time to realize. He was sick, or felt like he might be sick. He needed to use a bathroom somewhere, but this pissed Max off. Max flicked a cigarette butt at Roland and it bounced off his chest, a shower of orange sparks raining down on the ground. There were people everywhere. At first it seemed like they were going to fight about it, about the cigarette, but then Max had his arm slung around Roland's shoulders and they were both laughing their asses off, stumbling around the square.

The next place was cramped, but they were playing Judas Priest's *Painkiller*. The walls were painted red and the ceiling was high. The bartender was a big guy with a shaved head who, as it turned out, used to play bass for a tech-death band in Indiana. Small world. He recognized Max, told him he really loved those first three Angelus Mortis albums, had them all on vinyl still, first pressings, not that back-on-black reissue bullshit, and then proudly claimed that all sorts of famous musicians drank in his bar, that Jaz Coleman was here just last night and had to be dragged out kicking and screaming after last call. Max's pride seemed a little wounded, grumbling about his early albums just being OK, that people thought too highly of them, that he'd done a lot of good work since those. Drinks were on the house. The knot in Roland's guts started to ease up a bit. So far it seemed like pretty much everyone spoke English. Roland couldn't remember meeting even one person who was from Prague, or *Praha* as they called it. He'd picked that up quickly, that he should call it *Praha*. Everyone seemed like they were from somewhere else, just passing through Praha on their way back to whatever hole they'd crawled out of. They met an Australian with arms like a superhero and a long, braided ponytail; two fat dickheads from Manchester who called Roland a fairy and laughed until they were red in the face when he said he kinda liked the Stone Roses; a beautiful and exotic couple from some exotic island country Roland had never heard of and instantly forgot the name of who'd just gotten married and were on their honeymoon.

One minute Roland felt like he had to throw up, the next he was riding high on a wave of euphoria. He leaned over the bar and yelled at the bald guy from Indiana. "Hey, you seen Max?"

The bartender looked pissed, said that Max had taken off. And then it was last call and the lights were on and Roland was out in the street in front of the bar, with no idea how to get back to the pension, no idea where Max had gone. He didn't recognize any of the people standing around smoking cigarettes. How was that possible? Where had everyone gone? Where the fuck was Max? Roland walked a ways and then threw up in front of a storefront. There weren't any alleyways around here to disappear into. So he just puked where he stood—and was glad he did. Throwing up cleared his head. He felt cold for the first time that night and zipped up his jacket. If he could find the Vltava, he'd be able to get going in the right direction. He made his way to the Astronomical Clock—the same clock the Australian had gone on and on about all night, telling Roland more than once how it was the oldest in the world—and bummed a cigarette off a dead-eyed kid in a soccer jersey. The square was still filled with people, even at this hour, though maybe not as many as earlier. Everything smelled like hot dogs. He stared at the clock until the cigarette burned down to the filter. He hoped to see the figure of death ring its little bell. He couldn't remember what time the Australian said it would ring its bell. His thoughts were jumbled. It was obviously on the hour. But he didn't want to wait around that long. He was freezing. The idea of a clock that featured the figure of death, a skeleton, to remind you that your time was gonna come, it cracked Roland up. He walked for about fifteen minutes before he came to the river. It was as if every light in the city had been turned up to ten, rippling on the oily black waters, as sluggish and gorgeous as molten gold. Roland followed Vltava back down south, blindly hoping he was going the right way. Eventually he passed the KFC, its windows darkened, door locked, and knew he was on the right track.

The starless and cloud-rippled sky glowed red and Roland wondered about the people who built the Astronomical Clock, whoever they might have been, the sheer amount of ingenuity and patience and attentiveness that must have gone into setting the astronomical dial. How many nights had they spent staring up at the nighttime sky? Tracking the movements of celestial bodies? How had they even known what they were looking at? Or what it all meant? How many hours had it taken to calibrate the clock's inner workings—its gears and chains and whatever else was in there—to make everything come together and show—show what?—nothing less than the way the whole universe turned in on itself and pushed and pulled and kept it all together and moving in a divine rhythm. It seemed like such an absurd thing for anyone to have done, and then on top of all that, as if that wasn't madness enough, to add the little skeleton ringing its fucking bell—

Roland bent over and threw up again, only this time he felt an onrush of cold blackness come with it, and the city street suddenly seemed so far away, twirled off into oblivion.

3

It was the same thing Max had been hearing for more than fifteen years. First, there was a compliment, something patronizing, then the word *especially*, and then the real truth, like a twist of the knife.

Yeah, man, I love your music—it means everything to me—especially those first three albums.

He'd hoped this trip to Europe would clear his head, maybe clear out some of the junk in his veins, too, get him into a better creative space, a healthier space, get him out of Chicago for a bit. The grind of that place was really starting to take its toll. He was using more than he wanted to be using, burning bridges left and right. He couldn't help himself. When things were going bad, he wanted to hurt people. It made him feel better when he made other people hurt. It was simple, really. But lately he'd been fucking over too many people too fast. It was all catching up with him, a crushing black wave looming overhead, threatening to crest. And so he couldn't believe his luck when his new label asked if he'd be interested in coming out to Europe. The timing couldn't have been better. He was likely to rip somebody's head off soon. Yet here he was, halfway across the world, listening to some blowhard, from Indiana of all places, some bald dickhead who used to play bass for some unsigned, shitty tech-death band no one had ever heard of, feed him that same tired old bullshit. *Those first three albums.* He'd never get out from beneath their shadow, would he? They haunted him. Christ, he was only seventeen when he recorded *Henosis* on a four-track in his mom's fucking basement, smoking shitty weed, worshipping Burzum like a hundred other greasy losers. He'd barely known how to tune his guitar back then. What was so special about that? There had been no vision in those days, no purpose. All the work he'd put into expanding the band's sound since then, experimenting with songwriting, studio effects, paying out the ass for more polished production, seeking out young and talented musicians to collaborate with, kids who needed a break, and for what? For more middling fucking reviews? What was the point if people only ever cared about those first three fucking albums? It made his fucking head hurt.

All of that work, everything he'd striven for—it was wasted energy. A waste of everything he had inside.

Max gave the Indiana-tech-death guy his best psycho stare, watched the color drain right out of the fat piece of shit's face. Yeah, asshole, you just pissed off the wrong fucking guy. Dickhead knew he'd fucked up, too. Drinks were on the house—by way of apology. What a fucking worm. Max clapped the guy on the shoulder and couldn't help but relish when he flinched. He'd only wanted to come in here, to this cramped and tacky tourist bar, because he was bored with the kid and they were playing *Painkiller*, which was a kickass album. The kid was wasted and acting like a douche bag, chatting up every anonymous asshole in the bar, spilling drinks, laughing too loud, bumming cigarettes. It was an embarrassment.

Max watched the way Roland moved through the bar, imprecise in his movements, unaware of his gargantuan size, the way people seemed to slink away from him when he talked too loudly. He wondered if he'd made a mistake recruiting him.

But damn, the kid could really slay on the drums. Wasn't a bad guitar player either, was rumored to have decent songwriting chops, too.

As much as he hated to admit it, he needed the kid's help.

Fuck it. He'd had enough. Time to go.

Max got the bartender's attention and then gave him the finger, mouthed the words *fuck you*, watched the dickhead's face crumple with confusion and rage, and then pushed his way through the bodies standing between him and the door.

He got in a cab, told the driver to drop him off at the metro stop in Kobylisy—way the fuck out at the edge of the city. Max lit a cigarette even though the driver asked him not to, just pretended like he didn't understand, another dumb and drunk American. What's that you say? I'm sorry, I don't understand. These guys had a chip on their shoulder because they used to be communists, and now they were playing catch-up with the rest of the free world, racing to oblivion. Big-screen TVs, CD players, cheap laptops, smartphones. Everyone in the world hated Americans because deep down inside, they wanted to be Americans. You didn't have to travel far to figure that out. First time Angelus ever played Wacken Open Air, first time he met European fans, other musicians, he'd figured all that out quickly enough—it was in their eyes, the kind of thing you can't hide— admiration and envy all mixed together.

Max zoned out on the bleary lights in the distance and let the alcohol flow through his veins. He'd need something stronger soon. He could feel the sickness clamping down onto his bones. The cab lurched around a tight corner and slid to a stop. Max handed over a few koruna and slammed the door as the driver started chewing him out in Czech. Everywhere in the world, it's all the same—people were just waiting to explode. Anger flowed through everything. That's what *Henosis* was all about for fuck's sake. Not what the Greeks had in mind, exactly, but it was the truth. The thing that unified us all—it was hatred. If only people would just accept it, embrace their hatred and learn to live with it, how much healthier things would be. We could drop all the bullshit and get mean. We could just be animals, lowdown and dirty.

That's what he needed to get back to. Albums that meant something, that had purpose. Those first three albums: *Henosis, Fields of Punishment*, and *Telos*. He needed to rediscover his purpose. It had to be something new, something he hadn't done before. A new vision.

The dark streets of residential Kobylisy were quiet, still. He heard the barking of a dog in the distance, threatened and guttural, its fury joined by another, the vicious sounds tangling briefly, culminating in a whine, a wounded silence. Max knew of a place nearby where he could get anything he wanted, anything at all, just had to make nice with an old friend. He could buy a fucking mortar shell if he wanted to—he didn't doubt it—those old Soviet connections. This wasn't the slick and rigged endgame capitalism of the States, everything packaged up and made in China and boring, nope, not here. Here, things were still reeling from the sudden vacuum created by the Velvet Revolution. These people had been plagued by the slow and stupid rot of communism long enough to truly hate the free world, or at least resent it enough to blindly mimic it with little enthusiasm. And who could blame them? So much of what had happened here throughout history had been beyond their control, the fate of their lives merely the result of expanding and collapsing empires, the Holy Roman Empire imposing its will on all of Central Europe, arrogant kingdoms built on blood swamps, the eruption of violence caused by revolt, then the slow decay that sets in before collapse, and finally the arrival of Germany's horrific war machine during World War II, the city of Prague spared Hitler's mania only because he considered it too beautiful to destroy.

Max came to a dark and narrow tenement house at the end of the street, tucked between a slick stone wall and a derelict storefront, its windows boarded up and painted black. He knocked at the door, squatted down, and, speaking through the mail slot in his broken Czech, batted back the sluggish questions asked of him. A few moments later, the door swung open, giving way to a long, unlit hallway. A dreadlocked kid, sausage-fingered and pale-skinned, hopped off his shabby wooden stool and patted Max down, told him that he apologized, that he was a big fan, that it was just a formality, that Max and any of his friends were always welcome. At the end of the hallway was a steep staircase, and at the top of the stairs, another hallway. Max passed a few open doors, a few darkened, cavernous rooms, reeking of opium and sweat. The door at the end of the hall swung open as Max came to it, an aging punk in studded leather standing in the threshold, her head shaved, lipstick dark red—Agnes. She held a heavy chain in her hand, which was leashed to the collar of a stubby red-nosed pit. The dog watched Max closely with yellow eyes as he stepped through the threshold, growled a lowdown and menacing growl. Agnes bent down and stroked the dog's muscular shoulder, shushed him. "He is a friend," she said, smiling at Max. She nodded at the dog. "We were just about to go on a walk."

The room smelled heavy with mildew and the walls were covered in brightly colored peeling and torn posters for old punk shows, faded band stickers, poorly Xeroxed political flyers. There were no windows and not much furniture either, just a shitty couch draped with a knit quilt backed up into the corner, an old refrigerator, a CD player on a chair. A single naked bulb burned and buzzed in the center of the ceiling. Agnes's band had been practicing here for as long as he'd known her.

"You actually live here now?" Max said. He couldn't remember how long it had been since he'd been here. Ten years? Agnes was thicker around the middle these days, sure, and her clothes looked a little tighter, a bit ridiculous for her age, her makeup heavier, but she was still beautiful, there was no denying that.

Agnes shrugged, crossed the room, the silver ring piercing her septum glinting in the light. She tied the dog's chain to the radiator. Judging by the thick cross hatches of claw marks gouged into the faded wood floor, this was a regular practice. Max didn't see a food bowl or water dish anywhere. "Sometimes I live here," Agnes said. "Sometimes I don't. Sometimes I am living in the van. Other times the youth hostels, even though I am not so young. It doesn't matter to me."

"And Pyotr?"

The dog slid to the ground with a heavy sigh, yawned, keeping its eyes trained on Max.

She looked at the dog. "He is bored with your questions." And then, "Sometimes he lives here. Sometimes he doesn't. We're all just coming and going." Agnes opened the fridge and removed two glass bottles of Coke, peeled off the caps with an opener screwed into the wall nearby, and handed one to Max. "You can relax. Your eyes give you away. Pyotr is in Moscow."

"Permanently?"

"No, not permanently. Is this what you came here for? To ask about Pyotr?"

Max took a sip of Coke, felt it pleasantly burn his throat. He held the bottle up. "This is what you guys worked so hard for? Tearing down your oppressors? To stock your fridges with this shit?" He took another sip. "Man, it is good, though."

Agnes ignored him. "I've read that you're going to Ukraine.

That the mighty Strigoi will record an album with Wisdom of Silenus. Pyotr knows them, sells them things they need. He does not like them—says they are not good people. He believes Seph is dangerous."

Max sat down on the couch, the smell of dust rising all around him. "Pyotr would know, right? The fucking prick." He ignored that all-knowing look on her face. "It doesn't matter if they're good people or not. I don't care about that. They're the only people left who are making the kind of music I want to make. Real black metal. I know that sounds stupid. Don't look at me like that. You make fucking punk music, so what the fuck do you know?"

Again, she shrugged. "Nothing much, I guess. I know how to make power chords. Scream about Ronald Reagan, tanks rolling down the street. That's all that punk music is to you, right?"

He took down half the Coke in two, three gulps, felt it fizz up in his mouth, push out and slide down his chin. His eyes watered from the pleasant, fizzy burn. He wasn't used to drinking shit like this. "You know," he said, "this room was the first place I ever shot heroin."

"They make pornos here now," she said. "For the Internet. On that very couch you're sitting on. The girls are young, sixteen, seventeen. They have tattoos on their necks. They're poor. Come in from the suburbs. Sometimes they come from as far as Estonia. Very pretty with long hair and their nails done. But too thin. They make enough money to buy new clothes, eat McDonald's, pay the cell phone bill. It's no life."

"And you get a cut, too?"

"Naturally."

"Very punk of you."

"The world is always changing itself, Max. It's not 1992 anymore."

Max thought about this for a few moments. She was right, of course. She knew that he couldn't let go of the way things were. But all of that was over. That's why he was here. He was taking the next step, moving on. Fuck those first three albums. He was going to make something new, something real. The fizz from the Coke made him feel lightheaded. He wondered if he might actually be drunk. It was difficult to tell sometimes. It didn't matter. What mattered was the sickness and the sickness was becoming difficult to ignore. "I puked all over myself," he said. "The first time I shot up. Threw up and passed out."

"You're much stronger now," she said.

"That's one way of looking at it."

"They murdered their drummer, you know."

"What? Who?"

"Wisdom of Silenus. Their drummer Falchik. He disappeared. The rumors go that they stabbed him and buried him in the woods. Of course, no one has seen anything, no one knows who did it. No one knows anything. And so it remains a mystery. Pyotr thinks that it was Seph who put the others up to it."

"Why would she do that?"

"Drugs. Seph likes to keep the compound clean and apparently this Falchik was bringing in drugs. Well, Seph didn't like that too much."

Max felt his pulse quicken. This last detail made him a bit nervous. He'd have to kick the shit before they left Prague. Shouldn't be too hard—there was still plenty of time. Maybe he could even wait until they left Bucharest. He'd done it before, he could do it again.

Agnes came over and sat down on the couch next to Max. She lit a cigarette and sat and smoked. Then she reached over and slid her small hand into his, surprising him. Her nail polish was chipped. She had a crude tattoo of a spider in the webbing between her thumb and first finger. "I'm happy you are here," she said. "I'm surprised to hear myself say this—but it's true. Seeing you brings back many happy feelings. And later, you'll leave, go to the next city, and meet up with another woman from your past, and it will be like this never happened."

"That's such a bad thing?"

"No, not such a bad thing at all. Easier maybe."

Across the room, the red-nosed pit was lying on its side, snoring softly. Agnes looked at the dog with a fondness that Max found weirdly beautiful. She'd looked at him like that once, years ago. He still remembered.

"Are you holding?" he asked.

She turned to him and smiled. "So that's why you're here." She exhaled her smoke and—just barely, in a manner perhaps apparent only to those who knew her best—shook her head with disappointment. "I should have known."

"You have no one to blame but yourself."

"You always did like to blame the victim." She looked him in the eye. "Max, you must promise me that you will be careful. You don't know Seph. You don't know any of these people. They are dangerous."

"Well then maybe I should check out the armory," he said, "see what Pyotr has in stock. Maybe get something to defend myself, you know?" He grabbed her wrist. "But first I wanna get fucked up."

She nodded.

"And make sure it's strong shit," he said. "After all, it's just like you said. I'm much stronger these days."

4

Roland woke up in his bed at the pension, still in his clothes, crusted puke all over his boots. The room lurched into focus. He actually heard himself gasp, as if he'd emerged from some inescapable nightmare. Waking up, it always felt like he was just barely escaping something awful, some terrible, alternate reality just beyond consciousness, a maze with no exit.

The door leading out into the hallway was wide open, and Max's bed was empty, sheets still tucked in neat and tight. There was no telling what time it was, but the sun was up. He went out and got a coffee from one of the cafés down the street. There wasn't much he remembered from the night before, just the bar with the red walls and the high ceilings. Judas Priest. Everything else came back in images, two-dimensional moments frozen in time—Max with a chicken bone clamped between his teeth, the shower of orange sparks raining down from his jacket, some kid in a bright-red soccer jersey—and that was pretty much it. The last two days were creeping up on him. He couldn't remember the last time he'd brushed his teeth. His head pulsed with a sickening ache. The rubbing-alcohol smell of Russian Standard was still in his scraggly beard. Roland couldn't stomach the coffee. It tasted like shit and he was starting to get a headache, feeling jittery. He ordered a beer instead. Then another. Ten minutes later, he was feeling fine. He was always alone, wasn't he? So what? He liked being alone. He fucking loved being alone. More time to think, to figure out his thoughts. The big problem with people was that they never took enough time to figure themselves out. They just went from one moment to the next and never took the time.

He didn't know what to do or where to go—no fucking way was he waiting around for Max at the pension, selfish bastard—so he went wandering back to the touristy part of town, and eventually started following signs that advertised a museum of medieval torture. That sounded pretty cool. Max wanted to find inspiration for the new album? This seemed like a pretty good place to start.

This wasn't going to be like Chicago. He wasn't going to go hunting for that asshole. Let him rot in a hole somewhere if that's what he wanted.

The museum wasn't much bigger than a single-family apartment, all narrow rooms, separate compartments, and warped hallways—and it seemed like no one else was there. The rooms were painted bone white, carpeted blood red. Roland paid the admission fee to the uninterested old man behind the partition and passed through the entranceway. There was a large wooden chair, its backrest and seat cushioned with massive, rusty nails. There was an iron pyramid attached to a thick metal pole. Hanging on the wall nearby was a framed illustration of a man straddling the pyramid, his face contorted by pain. From there, it got weirder and weirder. Roland took it all in hungrily. The hallways seemed to go on and on, one room leading to another to another. Was there really no one else here? There was an iron maiden, a gridiron, all manner of chastity belts, torture masks, bone saws—they even had a full-sized rack. Everything looked legit, the metals layered with patina, leather straps believably cracked and worn. The final room led to a narrow staircase that went down into the basement. A hand-drawn sign was tacked to the low overhang, displaying an old-fashioned guillotine with the words "Watch your head!" written in English. Roland ducked beneath the sign. The staircase was deceptively steep, vertigo inducing, each wooden board creaking beneath his heavy boots. He wished he'd eaten breakfast.

The basement had been done up in the style of a castle dungeon, fake stone walls made out of plaster and Styrofoam creating narrow passages, the ceiling painted black, prison cells on either side. Inside the cells, behind rubber bars spray-painted black, were freakishly lifelike re-creations of torture scenes.

The only light came from fake sconces on the walls, shitty fake candles, orange and glowing. Pre-recorded sounds—howls of agony, pleas for mercy, the occasional and rhythmic cracking of a bullwhip—blasted from speakers mounted in the ceiling beams. The first cell showed a man strung up by his feet, hanging mere inches above a pit of red-hot coals. The next featured a motionless blade that looked suspiciously like the titular mechanism in "The Pit and the Pendulum," or at least Roger Corman's adaptation of that story. The blade dangled a few inches above a cheap rubber dummy. Both exhibits were unimpressive. The wax faces looked terrible, smudged and lacking human emotion. But then the narrow passage opened up to a detailed depiction of a man being drawn and quartered. This was much better, way gorier. Roland studied the way the horses' nostrils seemed to flare, so lifelike, he could almost feel their breath on the back of his neck, the realism of their packed and rolling muscles and the warmth of the light on their fake coats, like Caravaggio's *Conversion*. As if echoing his thoughts, the sound of galloping—coming closer, now almost right behind him—came from the speakers. Roland fought the urge to dive out of the way. His nerves were shot, apparently. Too much booze. He laughed at himself and realized, for the first time in months, he felt free, unburdened by all the negative bullshit that followed him like a dark cloud.

Last, he came to an exhibit that showed a man strapped to a wooden breaking wheel, one arm pinned to his side, the other hideously fractured, twisted over his head. Both of his legs were bludgeoned, bruised. The torturer, face hidden behind a sackcloth hood, readied his club once more. This one was so lifelike it was actually scary. Weirdly compelled, Roland leaned over the velvet rope partition to get a better look at the face of the victim. He had to admit that it sort of looked like him—more than sort of, actually. It was an uncanny likeness. He took a step back, taking in the whole exhibit again.

He read the wall label, which said that the wheel symbolized great dishonor, that the victim was often destined to come to no good. The whole thing left a negative impression in Roland's mind, God knew why, like a bad fucking omen.

He made his way back upstairs and noticed that the old man was gone. He didn't bother stopping in at any pubs on the way back to the pension. He didn't think his stomach could handle any more alcohol. He kept hoping he'd see something horrible. He wanted to see someone get stabbed, a mugging, one of those chanting groups of English hooligans beating on someone, snarling like dogs. But nothing happened. Everything stayed boring as it ever was. Everything was always boring. It was just starting to get dark and the air was much colder than the night before. He bought a loaf of bread from a market, broke it open, ripped out soft chunks with his fingers. The bread calmed his stomach.

Soon enough he heard riffs taking shape, bubbling up through his thoughts like a primordial ooze, a few notes at first, finding their rhythm, and then a complete bar. It always started like this—with a riff. Then a tremolo line. And these two things would always complete their circle, synch up, meet back at the beginning. He let the patterns emerge all on their own, hearing out the riff again and again and again. The song would evolve. The tempo would slow. He imagined the song being born like a planet, one layer at a time. And then he remembered the Astronomical Clock, the patience and discipline required by those who had mapped out the universe. And from this thought the map of the song spanned his mind. Roland saw the loops of its passages orbit one another like planets locked in an interstellar dance.

He would not rush this song. It would have the weight and persistence of gravity itself.

Moments like this were rare. There would be more parts to work out later, of course, the parts of songwriting that were difficult, tedious, the utility of the whole thing, the transitions, the melody. But for now, he had the shape of the thing, the tone—the idea of it.

As he climbed the stairs to their room, he knew that Max would be back, almost as if he could feel his presence behind the door.

The room was dark, quiet. Roland shut the door behind him and turned on the light. Max sat shirtless at the small table near the TV, his head lolled forward, chin on his heavily tattooed chest, hair hanging in front of his face. His belt was still cinched around his bicep. He was snoring softly—so he definitely wasn't dead. Roland undid the belt and let it drop to the floor. He turned on the TV—muted the sound, flipped around until he found some kind of a call-in show, a stunningly beautiful naked teenage girl alone in a room, phone pressed to her ear—and sat on his bed, took off his shirt but left his boots on. The girl was skinny, with round, bony hips. Her nipples were pale. Her small breasts were perfect. She seemed so unbelievably bored. All of the women in this country seemed beautiful and bored. He smoked three cigarettes, then turned off the lights and sat up in bed, watching the girl on TV soundlessly talking into the phone, the call-in number flashing at the bottom of the screen.

He thought about what he might say to her, what they would talk about, if he called in. The thought of it made him almost unbearably sad. He was always alone. He hated being alone. Too much time to dwell on everything that was wrong. That had always been his problem. He always had too much time to sit and dwell on what was wrong.

Roland got out of bed and walked to the table. He dipped his pinky into what was left of Max's heroin and bumped it. Fuck it. He'd never know.

It was better shit than Roland had ever had, stronger. He couldn't feel his face. The nausea was overwhelming and it was instant. He got back into bed and watched the naked girl on the TV, fighting the overwhelming urge to puke. His skin was an all-encompassing, impossible itch. In his worst moments, time always seemed to stretch out, become interminable. He turned this thought over again and again in his mind, with difficulty, finding it increasingly elusive, slippery, shedding bits and pieces each time he found it once more, until it was all but gone, leaving him forlorn, utterly and impossibly alone.

5

Max bought their tickets on an outdated computer in a shitty little Internet café near the pension. The computer was slow and loud and the website difficult to understand, but with a little help from the girl behind the counter, he'd managed. As expected, Roland proved utterly useless, just hung out in front of the café, burning through his cigarettes, slavering at the frightened women who walked by. Everywhere Roland went, it seemed, he made people uncomfortable, always staring, breathing through his fucking mouth, always standing in the way. Max printed out the boarding passes and paid with the label's credit card. The trip was eight hours—a night train—and they'd have to share a sleeper. No big deal. They'd been in each other's space for two nights now. It'd gotten to the point that Max was relieved to leave Prague behind. The kid was under his skin and festering. A little travel, some movement, would help take the edge off. Or so he hoped. As a gesture of goodwill, Max picked up a pint of vodka and offered to split it with Roland. They made their way to a little green park, just trying to pass the time before departure. Still the minutes crept by. After his first swig of booze, the kid smoked his last cigarette and asked Max if he could bum one. That gave way to another and then a third. The kid was the worst kind of mooch, thankless and expectant, a fucking baby. He wasn't sipping on the vodka so much as he was guzzling from it. When the bottle was empty and they'd run out of things to talk about—nothing outside of metal and horror movies—they took a cab to Hlvani Station and ate limp French fries drowned in mayonnaise. Max paid. The grease hurt his stomach and Max wondered if maybe he was developing an ulcer. Half an hour later they boarded the train.

First stop was Budapest, by way of Bratislava, where they were scheduled to spend two more nights pushing each other closer to murder, one step at a time. After that, there was the long and utterly dreaded train ride to Bucharest, the so-called Paris of the East, where they'd hole up for another night. And then finally a quick flight to Kharkiv. Max thought about Agnes, the way she spoke of Wisdom as if they were ghosts. If someone like Pyotr thought they were dangerous, well, truth be told, that did make Max a little nervous. That was why he picked up a blade and a few other things for protection. Maybe Agnes was just fucking with him. She did shit like that sometimes, just to get a rise out of people. Either way, Max was tough, he could take care of himself. No doubt about that. He'd hung out with some of the biggest freaks in metal. He'd gotten trashed with Maniac for fuck's sake. But he was starting to worry if the kid could hang, that they'd see him for what he was, an overgrown child.

As soon as they got to their compartment, Max received an email on his phone from Grigore Shevchenko, a guitarist for Wisdom, who agreed to pick them up from the airport in Kharkiv and drive them back to the band's compound somewhere north of the city. Max read the end of the email out loud to the kid. "I hope you brought warm clothes, it is cold here and we will be spending our first night in the forest beneath the stars."

"I've got flannels," Roland said, shoving his bag under the bottom bunk. "That should be enough. And my sleeping bag. And my leather jacket. I guess I could pick up a winter hat in the next city, whatever it is again."

"Budapest," Max said, bristling.

"Whatever." Roland pulled shut the window curtain. "My head's fucking killing me," he said, sliding into the bed and lying on his back. He never took his boots off, Max noticed, even when he slept, like they were fused to his big, goofy feet.

The sleeper was even smaller than he'd thought it would be, extremely cramped, already reeking of Roland's filthy boots, the scalpy smell of his unwashed hair. Max's stomach was really starting to give him some fire. He took a deep breath.

"You should have brought a hat with you to Chicago," he said. "It's the middle of fucking December."

The kid covered his eyes with his arm. "How the fuck was I supposed to know? I'd never been there before."

Because it's common fucking sense, Max thought, holding his tongue.

After a while, Max felt the train as it pulled away from the station silently and smoothly, gradually building up speed. He didn't remember the trains ever being this modern in Europe. He felt like he was forgetting so much lately.

Once it was apparent that Roland wasn't going anywhere, Max wordlessly left the sleeper and made his way down the narrow passage leading to the silent car. He passed two men in shirts and ties tapping away at sleek laptops, a wide-eyed teenage girl glued to her smartphone, her delicate skull engulfed by a pair of massive headphones, and a stunningly beautiful older woman reading a paperback, something highbrow probably, stuffed up, something in German. Beyond the large windows, a dismal and dreary suburban landscape whisked by, all washed-out color, small houses and narrow roads. The train glided along the tracks smoothly, nearly silent, its gentle swaying barely noticeable. He was about to push through the sliding doors and into the next car when he saw the placard on the wall that said smoking was prohibited throughout the train. Fucking unreal, right? Last time he'd traveled through Europe, maybe four or five years ago, it had seemed like every passenger smoked. Or maybe he'd just been in a smoking car? He couldn't remember. It had certainly seemed that way, at least, the way he remembered it. He really was having a hard time remembering things lately, smudging or fudging the details, names and circumstances emerging all on their own from a swirling fog. Max went back to the silent car and slumped against the window, bummed the fuck out, plugged his earbuds into his phone. He flipped through his library and selected one of his own albums, *Telos*. He almost never listened to his own stuff because all he heard were the things he should have done differently. This was still the case. At the time, he thought his third album would be his final statement on everything—the end goal. That hadn't exactly been the case. Now the music just didn't make sense to him anymore. He couldn't concentrate on what it was trying to say. The sounds drifted through his mind, nothing more than a sustained hiss. How was it possible that he was the same person who had made this? He felt like pulling his hair out. Instead, he got up and stomped back to the sleeper, angrier than ever.

He splashed cold water on his face and sat on the narrow seat lining the wall opposite the bunk, sat unmoving as the soft orange light bleeding around the edges of the curtain slipped to red to purple to blue. Then he had an idea. He pulled out both bags, opened them up. Then he dug out the shit he'd bought from Agnes and stuffed it all into Roland's bag, buried it beneath his stinking, crusty shirts and underwear. When he was done he zipped up both bags and shoved them back beneath the bunk.

Roland slept, oblivious, breathing loudly through his mouth. For a moment, Max wondered why he did the things he did, why he insisted on making everything harder than it needed to be. There was something wrong with him, he knew that much, but he was helpless to fix it, powerless as he watched one disaster after another explode in his face—and always of his own doing. He had front row seats to the shit show, each and every day of his miserable existence. He felt sick. He felt nothing at all beyond this sickness, lurking somewhere behind his eyes, pulsing dully. He wished he was dead. And then Roland snorted loudly, pulling in a jagged, apneal breath, and Max envisioned himself, for the first time since it had happened, on that late night in Chicago, straddling the kid's chest, wrapping his hand around Roland's throat. He'd wanted to kill him that night, he was sure of it, but he couldn't remember why. The thought of it made his palms sweat. He was losing control, blacking out more frequently. He hated to admit it to himself, but he was getting old, forgetful. And it was this idea of losing control that he feared more than anything else—not the damage that he might do, fuck that— but rather that he was acting outside his own sense of self-preservation, the only human behavior that Max considered to be truly insane. Because if you weren't all about taking care of yourself, then what good were you, really?

He felt the train slowing and then come to a stop, heard the loud, hissing release of the brakes. Soon afterward, a knock came at the compartment door, insistent. Max got up and let them in, foreign police, genuinely curious to see how this would all unfold.

He'd had a feeling this might happen—one of those moments of intuition. Oh, well, now it was Roland's fucking problem.

There were two of them, a man and a woman, here to conduct a standard passport check. They wore black boots, bulky gear-laden vests, gloves, and berets. Both had handguns holstered at the hip and their heavy equipment clanked and groaned as they entered the compartment. The man was older, with a silver moustache, piercing eyes, and the woman was young, short and stunningly pretty. They stood on either side of the cramped space, facing one another, the man in the doorway, the woman with her back to the window.

Max felt the way their eyes crawled over him. It always went down like this, wherever he went, the way people assessed him, quickly putting together what it all meant: his long hair, the tattoos on his hands and neck, the patches on his jacket, his boots. He wore the uniform of the metalhead, not uncommon at all in these parts of Europe, but still conveying misanthropy. It was a uniform every bit as much as their blue jumpsuits. But the actual wearing of a uniform isn't what's important—everyone does it one way or another—it's what the uniform says that's important, what it communicates to the rest of society. And police, their uniforms proclaimed loud and clear that they wielded the power to strip you of your personal freedoms for even so much as looking at them the wrong way. He hated them and he hated the people who sympathized with them. They were the scum of the earth, fascists one and all.

Roland was awake now, propped up on his elbows in bed, dazed. He looked from one officer to the other, then to Max. "What's going on?" he asked. Max ignored him. The compartment reeked of stale booze and sweat. The kid was sweating fear. Max idly wondered if maybe the kid had something to hide, something he didn't know about. And this thought made the situation all the more interesting because it was an unexpected development.

"Passports, please," the woman said.

"Of course," Max said. "Mine's in my bag." He gestured to the luggage stuffed beneath the bottom bunk, then to Roland. "So's his."

"You should have had them out and ready," the female officer said. "There was an announcement." She knelt onto one knee, her leather boots creaking loudly, and swiftly pulled each bag into the center of the compartment. She pointed to the bag closest to her. "Whose is this?" Max raised his hand. She looked up at him and nodded. "Remove your passport, please." Max did as she asked and returned to his seat.

She scanned his passport with some kind of device, a small computerized reader. Despite his controversial history, and the image he'd subsequently created for himself, Max had never actually been arrested, never been on probation, never issued a citation for public drunkenness, pissing in the street, or being in the park after dark. He'd never even gotten so much as a parking ticket. Luck had always been on his side. And it was this thought, that he'd always been lucky, that caused him to flash a smile at the female officer. She did not reciprocate.

With a surprisingly soft voice, the male officer politely asked Roland to retrieve his passport. Roland leaned over, unzipped his bag, and then straightened his back in a jolt, startled, as if he'd uncovered a nest of coiled snakes. Roland's eyes were wide and bright with surprise. He looked dumb, without reason. Max briefly fantasized about shoving his thumbs into Roland's eyeballs and pulling his skull apart.

There, lying on top of his dirty clothes, was the perforated metal handle of a butterfly knife, gleaming in the light, as well as an electric stun-gun.

"What the—" Roland began.

The male officer took a step forward into the compartment, leaned over slightly to get a better look at what was going on. Max watched all of this closely. Then the female officer pulled out two silver tear gas containers. The male officer's eyes flashed at his partner and the two exchanged an ever-so-slight simultaneous nod. Then he swooped down a long arm and quickly grabbed the bag out from under Roland. All of this happened before Roland was even able to finish his sentence.

"—fuck is this?"

The female officer had her hand on her pistol. Max saw that she had unfastened the thumb break snap. It was all happening so quickly and yet Max watched it all as if it were happening underwater. He lived for this shit, these moments. He felt alive. It was better than drugs. He closed his eyes and allowed himself to experience the moment in all its intensity. And when he opened them again, the moment had passed as all moments must. Roland was being led out of the compartment by the male officer. The woman stayed behind, talking into her walkie. Both bags had been taken for inspection. Max felt the blood pulse through his neck. He was coming down back into himself. And then later he knew he'd crash—and hard. But for now, not quite yet.

6

The cop raked all the garbage out of Roland's bag until it was strewn across the glaring metal table, a bummy smear of tatters, the only worldly possessions he could lay claim to. It was oddly embarrassing, witnessing someone go through his meager belongings—having to wear latex gloves no less—and doggedly sorting through his filthy and stained undershirts, his crusty boxer shorts, his book on art history, a pair of crappy headphones held together with masking tape, reeking socks, a few snot-caked bandanas. As if that wasn't bad enough on its own, the cop then pulled out a jet-black, tactical gas mask from the bottom of the bag, a perfectly new, perfectly unused gas mask that could not possibly have looked more out of place among the worn and wasted remnants of Roland's messy existence. After that he found what appeared to be a flash grenade.

"None of that shit is mine," Roland said. "That is obviously not mine."

"This is your bag—your belongings?"

"Yes, sir." Already he was talking to the cop as if he were his old man. He always did this with authority, deferred to it, went weak. Whatever it took to get off unscathed, make it all go away, that's what he did. Because he was a pussy. And it was his experience as a pussy that a little politeness went a long way

48

with a man in uniform. "It's my bag, that's correct. Everything in it is mine. Only not the tear gas and the gas mask. Or the knife. Or the—whatever else you found. I have no idea where those came from. Honest."

They stood on either side of the table in a cramped storage car near the end of the train. The lights overhead were harsh and buzzing. In the back of the car, a handful of small dogs barked and yapped from the safety of their kennels. Another officer slid silently into the room and stood near the doorway, hands resting on his belt. Beyond the door, out in the passage, Roland heard the hiss and crackle of a walkie-talkie. There were more of them out there, waiting to see what happened. They were worried that Roland might be a threat. It almost made him want to laugh, but he was too scared. Were they going to send him home?

Again, as he had done four or five times already, the cop asked Roland for his destination, the purpose of his visit. These were just tactics. Each time the cop repeated himself, he would then follow up with different, probing questions, like where Roland had grown up, his place of residence, his school, what he liked to do in his spare time—whatever.

"And the cuts on your hands?" the cop asked suddenly. "How did you get those?"

Shit. Roland absentmindedly rubbed his thumb over the knuckles on his left hand, feeling the slightly creased crisscrosses of newly healed skin. He recalled the meaty slap of bone on bone, the howls of pain followed by a spray of blood, a pink mist suspended in the air, the embarrassingly pathetic sounds of a grown man sobbing.

"A fight," Roland said. "It's a long story."

The cop waited expectantly.

"OK. Look, it happened in the States—before I even met up

with my friend. I told you I'm between homes? I was staying at a mission—a place where people can go to get off the street? They had us sleeping in beds in a gymnasium. It was crowded. I caught somebody going through my stuff in the middle of the night. That's all."

"That's all?"

I beat the living shit out of him, Roland thought. I crushed the guy's eyeball and cut my hands open on his busted teeth. I pounded his face until it went purple.

Of course that wasn't all. There was plenty more. Like how the guy who tried to rob him had a knife stuffed in his boot, or how it turned out that the guy was a serial rapist who had violated his parole. The cops showed up and the whole thing was swept under the rug because, really, who the fuck cared if some scumbag rapist got his face caved in? And let's be real, what the fuck did these assholes think he was going to do with tear gas and a stun-gun? Set it off on the train and jump out the fucking window? None of this made any sense. Was it even against the law to have tear gas? Roland had no idea. Max would know, of course—the old fucker seemed to know everything. And just like that, with no doubt in his mind, Roland realized that it was Max who had put the tear gas in his bag. It was Max. He was back in the sleeper laughing his ass off. But why? Why would anyone do this?

Roland felt like he was going to be sick, his itching hands cradling his molten stomach. They'd just started getting along these last few days. Hadn't they? The bruise on his thigh from when Max had kicked him—still there all these days later, brown and discolored like a bad apple—began to throb.

A pre-recorded announcement blared from the train's intercom system, apologizing for the delay, and assuring passengers that they would be moving shortly. Roland found himself desperately hoping that he would be among them. Even if it meant he had to go back and face Max. He didn't care. Maybe he'd even be able to laugh this whole thing off later. But for now—he had no idea. He had no idea about anything, really.

Please, shit, he never asked for anything. He really did not want to be sent home. He should have seen it coming. This was always the pattern in his life. Something good would happen and then something bad would come storming in and wash it all away.

There was another flare of hiss and crackle from the cop's walkie-talkie. He sighed deeply and looked Roland in the eye.

"If I let you go through," the cop said, pointing at him with a gloved finger, "you need to understand that your behavior, what you do while you are here, will reflect on me."

"Of course," Roland said, not quite believing—not letting himself believe—the sudden turn their conversation had taken.

"You cannot take any of the weapons. Or the tear gas. Those stay with us. You are allowed to keep the mask, however."

I don't give a fuck about the fucking mask, Roland thought. He kept his mouth shut, merely nodded. He then did as he was told, packed up his shit, and headed straight back for the sleeper compartment, still unsure why they'd let him go so easily. Whatever; it wasn't worth thinking about. As he passed row after row of other passengers, he felt them staring at him, muttering, and so he kept his head down and moved quickly. There's no way they could have known he caused the delay, right? Fuck it. Of course they knew. More than ever now, he was conscious of how he looked, how he was dressed, how other people saw him. He was trash. He was somebody to fuck with. Tears welled up in his eyes. His breathing was rapid, shallow. He popped the door open and saw Max sitting exactly where he'd left him, looking both weirdly worried and self-satisfied. What he wouldn't give to just bash the old fucker's head in. Instead, he threw his ratty bag on the floor and sat in the bed, facing Max.

"You are an asshole," Roland said, his voice flat.

It was like a vacuum had sucked all of the air out of the compartment. For a moment, Roland didn't know how Max was going to react. He was worried that Max was going to explode, stand up, and start screaming in his face. Or maybe he was worried that Max wouldn't react at all, would just stay silent and cool, offering no explanations. But what he didn't expect was for a sly grin to creep across Max's face.

It was just a prank, this grin said. Nothing more.

Max erupted with laughter, high pitched and manic. "You should have seen your face when they took you away," he said. "I thought you were going to shit yourself."

There was no way for Max to know that Roland was running from his past, right? There was no chance that Max was teasing Roland with this fact, reminding Roland that he could have him sent home whenever he saw fit, expelled back into the crushing machine of poverty and hunger. He couldn't be that cunning, that malicious. Right?

Max told him he'd spent some of the label's money when he was fucked up in Prague, bought a bunch of weapons. He must have stuffed them in Roland's bag by accident when they packed up at the pension, he said, laughing.

Roland was genuinely surprised to hear himself laughing, too. He was also relieved. He decided to swallow Max's bullshit. It was easier that way. And so he let that relief bleed into his laughter and carry away all the tension and hurt he felt.

The train barreled on into the blackness. Max went to the dining car and bought cans of cheap beer. They drank together, unwound. Roland even popped off his boots, stretched out on the bed. They talked about horror movies, repeating themselves, their familiar opinions, all of the things they'd already said earlier in the day, already professed, and it was comfortable because it was familiar, it was easy—no thinking necessary. They talked about metal. They talked shit about bands they both agreed were shit. They talked about the album they were going to make. Roland talked about the museum of medieval torture, the Astronomical Clock, how he saw it all coming together, and Max, for his part, seemed like he cared. He nodded along, said it sounded like Roland was onto something. And maybe he was, Roland thought. Maybe he really was. And so they kept drinking until the dining car stopped serving and then Max broke out the flask he'd stashed in his luggage and they drank some more. Pretty soon Roland was dead drunk, pissing in the sink every twenty minutes. And once or twice, even though he was dead drunk, Roland thought he saw something flash deep in Max's eye, a twinge of hatred and menace. And once or twice, the conversation hit weird lulls that gnawed at something in Roland's heart. But these lulls were easy to ignore; they were easy to cover up. It was just a matter of making noise, continuing to talk—taking another swig, taking another piss—saying whatever came to mind, whatever it might be, and not worrying about what it meant. But most importantly, it was about ignoring all the things they weren't talking about, the things Roland felt that he could not say—not to this person, the man who sat across from him in this cramped, stuffy room. Because more than ever, Roland knew that he did not know this person, he did not trust this person, he was not safe with this person. He would have to watch himself.

The train barreled on.

PART TWO
THE TRIUMPH OF
DEATH

1

Max and Roland arrived in Ukraine early in the morning, the blood-orange sun trembling on the horizon. Grigore Shevchenko picked them up at the airport, just as he'd promised. He was a big dude, as big as Roland, and he wore a black hoodie with cryptic band logos on the sleeves, combat boots, Siberian camo pants. His head was shaved and his eyes were mean.

"Welcome to Ukraine," he said. He braced Roland's shoulder with his free hand when they shook, letting him know he was in control. They stood eye to eye. Right away there was tension. But then Grigore smiled. "Come on—we have a long drive."

He led them to a white van, drove them an hour west and then far north. Impenetrable black metal blared from the van's speakers as the garish signs of civilization gave way to formidable expanses of dark wood. Twice they stopped at imposing metal gates and twice Grigore got out of the van and removed heavy padlocked chains so they could proceed.

As darkness fell, the road came to an end. "We go the rest of the way by foot," Grigore said. He instructed Max and Roland to take their bags—they would not be coming back anytime soon. Roland's energy was already flagging. There had been little to eat, an apple apiece, dry handfuls of flaky granola. Grigore had refused to stop for fast food, which he said was poison.

The moon-gleamed snow was clean as bleach, crunching beneath their boots as they pushed deeper into the forest, the sound of it crisp and brittle. And far above, the slate of nighttime sky was choked with blue-bright clusters of stars. Grigore led the way. Max and Roland lagged behind, sucking lung-shockingly cold air, doing their best to keep up with their guide. Grigore explained that this was something they did with all of the bands they worked with. It was tradition, a means of communing with the natural world in preparation for creating their art. The natural world, he said, was the key to everything. It was the source of true strength—man's inner essence—his soul. And that once a man lost touch with his soul, he was lost forever. This, Grigore said, was a fate worse than death.

Max said something under his breath about this being stupid, but Roland was into it. The fresh air reminded him of home, reminded him of Bellingham. It had been years since he'd taken a walk through the woods. He'd forgotten how much he missed it.

This forest was primeval, still, dense with conifers. Birch trees rose from the forest floor as stark as bones. Each time Roland passed between two of them, he imagined himself passing through a doorway. Some of these doorways he saw as entrances, others as exits, and all around him, the boundless and haunted dimensions of an unknowable labyrinth. They heard the laughter of a tawny owl.

The only other sounds were their cloudy, labored breathing, their boots crunching the snow. They'd been walking—hiking really—for more than an hour and tendrils of steam curled from Grigore's shaved head, but still his pace did not slow.

"How much farther is it?" Roland asked. His breath was ragged. He shifted his lumpy duffel bag from one shoulder to the other. His toes had long ago gone numb and the muscles in his legs were strapped and aching.

Grigore spoke over his shoulder, still moving. "Not long now," he said. "Keep up."

The tree line dropped away as they entered a large clearing and the sudden onrush of open space seemed to pull their momentum into a vacuum. It was a breathtaking sensation. Roland stood speechless as the sky expanded, deepening like a black portal. Max brushed past him, muttering something about a bad knee, his lower back, but Roland barely noticed. He was lost in himself. Grigore called to him now from far away, commanding him to catch up. The tread of his boots scraped against the ice as he scrambled up the steep incline of a rocky hill. He found his footing on jagged stones dusted with snow and climbed onto the mound's summit, breathless.

There, Grigore stood near a large wooden post, which leaned at an extreme angle. He reached forward and placed his hand on the ashen wood, which appeared as timeless and weathered as stone. He lowered his head slightly, closed his eyes, as if drawing strength from some magic monument. Max tried to catch his breath, hunched forward, hands on his knees.

It was some kind of marker, an alien structure in an otherwise barren landscape. The post was tall and strong as a tree, its base planted firmly within a deep crag in the stone. Mounted at its far end and laid flat was a large and oddly warped wooden wheel, which had collected quite a bit of snowfall—a breaking wheel, much like the one he'd seen at the museum in Prague. Past Grigore, he saw that the rocks gave way to a deep, snow-lined valley flooded with moonlight. And past this post were dozens of other posts, these mounted wheels, spaced evenly every hundred yards or so, some still upright, miraculously reaching toward paradise, others cracked and broken, their wheels lost to the ages. He'd seen posts like these before. Several of them were portrayed in Bruegel's *The Triumph of Death*, that grand portrait of the end of the world, of mankind meeting its fate at the hands of an army of lunatic skeleton warriors.

"They call this the Valley of Many Sorrows," Grigore said. "It is a place of great historical importance. I'm sure I don't have to tell you that very few outsiders have come this far. The wheels used to line the royal road that led to the high castle—a warning to those who might choose to disobey the law. Come, we do not have much more to travel."

They followed the line of breaking wheels down into the valley. All sound fell away, as if they'd entered a void of silence. There was no wind and the snow here was wet, sucking, the crunch of their footsteps swallowed whole.

All this talk of man's inner essence, of a fate worse than death, the sight of the breaking wheels, it put Roland on edge. He didn't like Grigore; he certainly wasn't comfortable around him. Outside of what he had read online, which frankly wasn't much, he knew very little about Wisdom of Silenus. He knew that they had a reputation for being bad people who made good music, that they had shadowy ties with the far right, and that they were tightly knit, secretive. In fact, they seemed to maintain zero web presence. Their official site, if you could even call it that, linked to something called the Pagan Alliance, which was really just a network of blogs and file-sharing sites that trafficked in mystical nonsense, Nazi lore, and off-the-grid black metal. They wanted to return Europe to its pre-Christian roots, despised organized religion of any kind, saw it as a hostile invasion. But Roland knew fuck-all about politics, and even made it a point to never hold anyone's beliefs against them, no matter how odious they might be. The world was a dangerous place and life was cruel, painful and pointless. One person's belief would never change that. Only hippies believed that anything would ever change, but they were the worst kind of hypocrites. As far as Roland was concerned, the smartest thing a person could do was expect the worst to happen at any moment. That way, you'd be ready for it.

They splashed through a shallow, rocky stream, its flowing waters crystal clear, and met a footpath that snaked through the light woods. Roland was glad he wore heavy boots. It was now getting quite late and the birch trees cast long shadows in the moonlight. A hare, or perhaps some other small and scared animal, kicked up powder scurrying into the frozen underbrush.

At the top of a hill stood a darkened cabin, its rambling frame against the sky, blacking out the shimmering light of the stars. It was like something out of a fairy tale, this small, dark house, a story for spooking children. Grigore leaned into its reinforced door with his shoulder, breaking it free from the cold. The cramped room smelled like soil, oiled leather. Max shut the door and, as Grigore instructed, clapped into place the wooden drop bar. Within a few moments, Grigore had a decent fire going in the brick-lined hearth, and the three men stood before the whipping, orange flame, thawing out their hands.

"We'll spend the night here," Grigore said. "Get comfortable."

Max unfolded a sleeping cot and dragged it across the packed dirt floor closer to the fire. Roland did the same. There was a pair of snowshoes mounted on the wall, an ancient hunting rifle, and an animal fur stretched out so large that it could only have belonged to a brown bear. Grigore tossed them both flannel blankets. Even wrapped up tight, the warm glow of the fire on his skin, Roland could not escape the cold. It seemed to be everywhere inside him.

The cabin had been built with the thick trunks of trees, the crevices between them packed with dried mud. The few windows, which looked like they'd been cut out with a chainsaw, were boarded up on the outside, tarped in clear plastic on the inside. And the shelves on the walls were stocked deep with cans of food.

Grigore bent down over the fire, affixing a cast-iron kettle to the pot hooks. Roland was beat. The sheer exertion of the journey quickly caught up with him and he allowed the warmth of the fire to lull him to sleep—until the screech of the kettle's boil called him back. They drank luxurious black tea, picked at salty chunks of dried fish with their aching fingers, and then lapsed into contented silence, mesmerized by the dance of the flame, shadows climbing up the walls.

"This cabin was built by fur trappers," Grigore said, breaking the spell. His eyes were sunken, pooled with darkness. "Each spring, when the snow melts, we make the necessary repairs. It has been done this same way since the old days, when man lived off the land."

Roland sipped his tea, relishing its smoky flavor. He was finally getting warm. He gestured to the fur on the wall. "Bear?" he asked.

Grigore's wide smile showed the spaces between his teeth. "That's right," he said. "The bear is the strongest animal of them all. To kill and eat a bear is an old aristocratic tradition in these lands. This one here didn't go down without a fight, either—gutted three dogs—weighed more than four hundred kilos. So legend has it. The hunter who killed him, Vasyl, he is a descendant of a very powerful family, the Drevylans, rulers from ancient times. The posts we followed earlier, they lead to the ruins of their castle. All of this—the lands, the trees—all of it is his." He paused. "There are very few of the brown bear left these days, I'm afraid."

There was a moment of silence. The fire crackled.

"Not many still practice the old ways," Grigore said. "They've been seduced by the modern world, which makes them fat and lazy. They have fallen under the spell of the leftist regime, so-called Judeo-Christian values. And they are quick to cannibalize their countrymen. But we seek to uphold the values and traditions that have made us who we are for centuries. It is what I said earlier—a man must maintain a connection with his inner essence—and a man's inner essence is reflected by his nation. The land he lives upon, it is his blood. In this, there is true strength." He looked at Max. "The music you made has been important to us and that is why you are here. Seph believes that, despite the fact that you are an American, you can make valuable contributions to our cause. She believes that you are spiritually connected to Wisdom, that you can help us get our message out there into the world."

Max nodded slightly, stayed silent.

Roland watched Max's face closely. He didn't know what Grigore meant when he referred to their cause, and he was all but ignorant of Ukraine's politics. Whatever Max might be thinking, his face did not show it. He sure was hard to read sometimes.

"How far are we from where we're going?" Roland asked. He wanted to talk about something else, anything else. The topic of conversation was too charged. And he worried that Max might say something stupid. They were out in the middle of nowhere. If things went south, Roland wouldn't know where to go—and it was freezing outside.

"The compound is a short walk from here," Grigore said. "It is quite an impressive place, you will see. It began only as an old farm. Seph spent the summers there when she was a girl. We brought in two shipping containers, built a bunker. Then we built the greenhouse. Now we have an entire community. We're wired for electricity. We have running water—even in the winter. We have our own laws. Our own way of doing things."

"Sounds idyllic," Max said, his voice soft, eyes lowered.

It didn't sound like Strigoi at all—not to Roland.

Grigore nodded slowly. "I can see that this kind of life appeals to you. That is what we expected. It's in your lyrics, after all. On your early albums. Strength in independence. The purity of the natural world. Yes, you will fit in just fine." He turned his gaze to Roland, smirked. "And you will, too, I am sure."

Maybe it was all in Roland's mind—it probably was, everything was—but there was something about Grigore's voice, something about the way Grigore spoke to him, that didn't feel right. His eyes said it all. You are not one of us. You will never be one of us.

2

Seph waited for her eyes to adjust to the darkness. The first cigarette in the morning was always the best and she allowed the pleasant blue smoke to fill the small room. It was the only vice she allowed herself, the one remnant of the outside world she couldn't let go of. She pulled on a pair of jeans, slid into rubber boots, and buttoned up an oversized flannel. A minute later and she pressed through the frozen mud on her way to the barn.

The morning air was bitter. She felt the skin on her face tighten.

This was the best part of her day, the only time she was ever alone. She grabbed a stool and a pail and set to work. First she milked the cows and then she milked the goats. When she was done, she checked in on Hecate, who, at ten years, was their oldest nanny. The goat paced her tiny straw-lined stall. Poor old thing was wide as a house and ready to kid at any moment. There wasn't enough space to separate the mother from her young, and that meant there was some risk that disease could spread from the baby through the milk. But that was a risk worth taking. More milk meant Seph could continue experimenting with raw uses. She was already quite good at making soap and lotion. And these two things went a long way toward restoring the comforts of life as it had been before she moved to the compound.

Not that she really missed the way things were back then. It was better out here. There was less stress, less noise. No dark-skinned immigrants, only white Europeans. Out here Seph was free to live the life she wanted to live. And the rewards for her hard work were shared only with those who deserved them.

In the beginning it had been just her and the other members of Wisdom: Roman, Falchik, and Grigore. Spooky Taras had materialized from God knew where and said he would stay for only a week, but that was two years ago. Now there were perhaps a dozen people living at the compound. There was Dusanka, who cooked, and Irena, who cleaned. There were the Russians—Pyotr, Ivan, and Oleh—who came and went as they pleased, sold them weapons at a reasonable price, and also brought valuable updates on the cossaks and the rebels, reports on where the worst of the fighting was taking place. And then there were the dozens of bands that paid to use the rehearsal hall, mostly just kids, skinny punks and metalheads who shouted artless lyrics about hating Putin or worshipping Nordic gods. The weekend-long festivals they hosted could sometimes attract as many as two hundred people. They were expecting at least that many at next week's Winter Solstice festival.

Everyone was expected to help out on the compound. You had to carry your weight, help plant crops, till soil, construct buildings. In exchange, you were given meals, weapons train-ing, and a place to sleep. In the summer, people slept in the cluster of trailers out in the fields. Once the cold set in, how-ever, those people would scatter back to wherever they came from, and fewer hands made things harder. But still, they had what they needed. They had food animals, chickens and rab-bits. They had solar panels powerful enough to charge a network of car batteries. They had generators and tools, high-volume water pumps and even gas lines. Most importantly they had enough firepower to lay low a small army. Because once the outside world ground to a halt, or the Russians moved up from Crimea and into their homeland—and Seph had no doubt that one of these two things would happen soon enough, perhaps one signaling the other—no one would be able to take what was theirs, at least not without first suffering heavy losses.

Some days she thirsted for war, for bloodshed. Other days she was content to create music. Still other days she was content to milk the cows and the goats. It all depended on the passing of the storms that raged within her.

But still, she had a job to do. She had to stay focused, in control.

Coming back from the barn, she passed Taras on his way to the chicken coop. He looked like an old mystic shrouded in his black hooded cloak, his thin beard barely visible beneath a cloud of tar-heavy tobacco smoke. He asked her about Hecate and she told him that the old goat was restless, that she was likely to go into labor by nightfall.

He nodded, spooky, always knowing more than he let on. "Last night," he said slowly, "I read the stones and spent a great deal of time interpreting thurisaz—a warning of the devil. If the goat's young is born with black fur, it will be a sign. The outside world is closing in."

"You're worried about the Americans," she said.

He merely shook his head.

Of course he was. They were all worried to one extent or another. But there was little to be done about all of that now. The deal had been done and the money had come in from Strigoi's label, more than Seph had seen in years, enough to buy a new industrial generator, a new tractor, MREs to last a year. They were adamant that he write an album here, whoever they were. It would be a legendary collision of two worlds, they said. History would be made.

Besides, she was eager to meet the famous Strigoi. And soon enough, she did.

They came in through the gate on the dirt road. The Americans were clearly exhausted, red faced and half frozen. Even though it was grueling, Grigore insisted their guests hike through the forest, no matter that there was a service road for the trucks that led directly into camp. They needed to make the journey, get a sense of where they were in the world. They needed to appreciate the country in all its greatness. This was holy land, land untouched by the foul and rotting hand of Christ. Many centuries had come to pass under the watchful eye of the Lord. Much blood had been spilled and many sacrifices made. Remaining connected to this history was their only way of honoring the dead—the many.

Strigoi was much smaller than she'd imagined. He had a delicate frame and a beautiful face, almost like a woman's. He was also clearly sick, probably from gypsy dope. She'd seen it before, with Falchik. But Strigoi wouldn't find any dope here, not anymore. She'd heard stories about his junkie behavior. He'd have no choice but to get clean, figure it out on his own, however painful that might be. The drummer he'd brought with him, on the other hand, looked strong as an ox, boyish, but stupid. His smile was innocent.

As she introduced herself, she paid close attention to the way each of them looked at her. Seph knew that she was beautiful and, despite her slight frame, she also knew that she exuded power. Men were often scared of her and she relished their fear. It afforded her control and control made her feel more alive.

Strigoi looked her in the eye but only because he didn't want her to know that he was afraid. The drummer, on the other hand, did not return her gaze. His hand hung limp in hers. He was a boy.

She led them to the main hall, a pre-fabricated steel garage they'd equipped with a small kitchen. The walls were insulated and during the winter it was the warmest building on the compound. They sat at the long table, her and Grigore on one side, Max and Roland on the other. Roman and Taras joined them soon enough. One of the cooks brought out servings of stuffed cabbage, steaming hot. Seph watched the Americans eat. It was obvious that they did not appreciate the food. They ate quickly and loudly. Neither of them said thank you. They had no idea what amount of effort—what sort of sacrifice— went into growing and harvesting crops. They took it for granted that food should show up. They were far from home.

Tea was served. The Americans were bored, blinking their eyes like tired owls. Seph felt only relief when Grigore finally stood up and announced that it was time their guests retired to the cinderblock shed they'd be sharing for the foreseeable future.

Maybe it was unfair but she couldn't help but feel disappointment. For years she had imagined Strigoi as someone larger than life, more of a spiritual entity than a man, someone who would exude some kind of powerful energy, a real mystic. When she was still a teenager, she had spent countless nights in her bedroom listening to *Telos* on her headphones, fantasizing about the end of the world, about going out in a blaze of glory. She memorized his lyrics, taught herself guitar by playing along to that album. And yet now that he was here—a dope-sick little man who breathed loudly as he ate, smacked his lips, and did not even say thank you—she felt silly for believing that a man could ever be more than that. He was just a man and she had known many men. They were always the same, always disappointments.

What did she expect?

Hours later, it was getting dark when Grigore knocked on her door. Annoyed, Seph put down the book she was studying, an old paperback anthology of female Ukrainian poets. He entered her room, sat next to her on the bed, blocking out the lamplight, and quickly pulled his sweater over his head. The rigid lines of his muscles were deepened by shadow. He leaned over to kiss her and she turned her face.

"Not tonight," she said, suddenly self-conscious of the fact that she wore nothing other than a T-shirt and underwear, of the fact that he was so much bigger than her.

"What? Why?" He swiftly pulled off his boots—first one, then the other—dropping them loudly to the floor. He reached for her breasts and she pushed his hand away. This seemed to genuinely surprise him, as if her body belonged to him. "It was freezing out there, you know," he said, sounding wounded. "And you had this warm bed all to yourself." He smiled at her, an attempt at levity perhaps. But it only served to make her angry.

"I was reading, you know—before you barged in."

"You've never minded my barging in before."

"Tonight I mind."

He seemed so ignorant sometimes, so pigheaded. Had he completely forgotten their understanding? She suddenly felt furious, a flash of primitive and deadly heat erupting from deep down. She wanted to lash out, but she also didn't want to hurt him. And yet he must understand his place in her life. He must understand that no one shared her bed with her unless they had been invited to do so. It did not matter if he had been invited the night before. It did not matter if he would be invited the night after. The only thing that mattered was now. And now, in this moment, he wasn't listening to her. Nothing in the world made her angrier than when she was ignored, when she spoke and was not listened to, because she was not one of those pathetic women who allowed herself to be ignored.

"It's him, isn't it?" Grigore said, his low voice sounding somehow both resigned and mocking. "The drummer." He actually rolled his eyes, the *bovdur*.

"You don't know what you're talking about."

"I saw the way you looked at him, out on the road. I know that look."

He was right, of course. She hadn't even realized it until he'd said it, not really, but he was right. She wanted the drummer and she knew that soon she would have him. Even admitting this to herself made her resent Grigore. She resented him for being right. She resented him for making her feel so obvious, so transparent. But mostly she resented him because he knew her so well, because he was so close to her.

"Nobody belongs to another person," she said. "I am free—"

"I know, I know," he said. "You are free to make your own decisions and sleep with whomever you want to sleep with." He swept up his sweater from the floor, exhaled deeply, looking straight ahead at the wall, away from her. "It does not matter. Eventually, he'll return to the States—and I'll remain."

"Yes, you will," she said, leaving it at that. Of course he'd still be there—nearby, available—just like he'd always been there, no matter how many drummers came and went. So why did he feel the need to state the obvious? Why now? She watched him put on his sweater. Then he pulled on his boots, began to lace them up.

"Strigoi is sick, you know," Grigore said. "It was a mistake bringing him here. I don't care how famous he is. People like him spread sickness."

She was about to say that she had noticed, that she wasn't an idiot, that Strigoi had been brought here because he was needed, that the Lord had told her so, when the knock came at the door, startling them both. Though his voice on the other side was muffled, she recognized Taras immediately. "Seph," he said, "you must come quick. It's Hecate."

The night was black, choking, the winds raising hell. Seph followed the sweeping beam of her flashlight to the barn. She swung the door open and the metallic stink of birth was inescapable. They went to the old goat's stall. Her young was already crowning. Even from a distance, Seph saw that the kid was positioned well, its head enveloped by an unbroken rope of blood-streaked mucus that swung close to the ground. Pinned beneath its head, a single delicate leg had also found its way.

Seph approached the pen slowly—Hecate seemed to pay her no mind—just in time to bear witness. The goat took a few tentative steps in her stall, ribs expanding and contracting with each labored breath, tail pointing straight in the air. With a convulsive push, Hecate squeezed the kid's shoulder free. And then the kid seemed to slide out all at once, tumbling head over foot onto the straw below where it lay heavy and motionless, gleaming wetly. Hecate immediately turned around, inspecting her young, giving its slick and steaming fur a few motherly licks.

Seph turned to Taras. "Its fur is brown," she said, almost laughing. "Not black." She felt a wave of relief wash over her, realizing only in this moment how much that stupid divination had weighed on her mind. She knew enough about runes to know that the reverse of thurisaz was an omen of good. Perhaps

Taras had gotten it wrong—

"Wait," Taras said. "The stones do not lie."

The kid lay still on its side. Something was wrong. It didn't appear to be breathing. Hecate doubled her efforts, licking the kid's head and neck, crying quietly. Seph's fingers curled around the cold top bar of the gate. With an animal's peculiar attunement to death, Hecate raised her head and let loose an almost human expression of grief. It was powerful and sudden enough to fill Seph with overwhelming sadness. She could hardly bear it. But still, she refused to look away. Because looking away would mean that she could not face the stark, unforgiving realities of the natural world. It would mean that she was weak.

Taras placed a heavy hand on Seph's shoulder. They did not speak.

The second kid was born perhaps fifteen minutes later, arriving with little resistance—its fur as black as night. No wonder Hecate had grown so large during her pregnancy. At first, it lay motionless in the straw just as its stillborn sibling had. Then it leapt to life, kicked its back legs as if passing an electric current, and expelled its initial weakened bleats. Hecate attempted to clean it, but the young goat proved difficult, thrashing its legs at its mother's face. It went on this way for quite some time, until finally the kid gave into exhaustion and went limp. And all the while, Hecate, poor thing, never stopped turning to the stillborn, as if expecting it to wake, to signal for its mother's help.

Taras entered the pen and gathered the dead in a blanket, cradled the tiny bundle tight against his chest, and told Seph that he would bury it in the old cemetery. Seph merely nodded in response. It wouldn't be the first corpse they had buried in the woods.

Black goats were born every day all over the world. Why should this one mean anything at all? It was only coincidence that Taras had interpreted the sign of the devil. It didn't mean anything—just superstition. The night winds slammed the barn door in its frame, clapping loud as hammer blows. In their rush, they'd left it wide open, letting out all of that heat, burning off all that expensive oil. How had she not noticed until now? Seph was just about to call out to Grigore to pull it shut when she realized that he had gone. But when had he gone? Had he even followed her to the barn? She couldn't remember him being there. No, only Taras had been there, his black presence as warm and comforting as a ghost.

3

Max spent his first night on the compound puking into a plastic bucket. The room was like a jail cell, cramped, bare concrete walls. They had a bunk bed and a small dresser for their clothes, some shitty shelves and a tattered rug. An ancient space heater glowed red in the corner, smelling of scorched dust. The lone window looked out upon a snow-swept, moonlit field. Outside, the wind was relentless, the sound of a door somewhere slamming shut over and over again. With generators occasionally roaring in the distance—the wind, the door slamming, the space heater's inhuman glow—Max felt like he was trapped in some kind of demonic machine.

"You alright, dude?" Roland said from the top bunk, voice disembodied in the dark.

A useless question. What the fuck did it sound like?

"I'm fine," Max said.

He sat on the floor, back against the bottom bunk, knees pulled close to his chest. He spit into the bucket. His head felt like a brick. If Seph or Grigore had noticed he was junk sick, they hadn't let on. Roland was probably just barely bright enough to have figured it out by now but he didn't give a shit about Roland. Either way, Max wouldn't be able to hide it much longer. He knew enough to listen to what his body was telling him. God, why hadn't he tried to smuggle something in? He was supposed to save the shit Agnes gave him… but he'd blown through it so quickly. At most, he had another two days before full-on withdrawal fell upon him. Then he'd be fucked—short of breath, muscle cramps, nightmarish anxiety and paranoia. He might even start shitting himself. It was always different, depended on how deep it got its claws into him. And even though he hadn't been hitting it that hard lately, at least not comparatively, he had no intention of finding out how bad it could get.

Roland softly snored. The sound of it sent Max crashing back into his body. How long had he been sitting here lost in thought? Fuck. It drove him nuts to think that the kid could sleep so calmly while he was forced to languish in misery. He let the bucket clatter to the floor, didn't care if the noise woke Roland up. Fuck Roland. Then he crawled into bed, shivering, sweating. Come morning he'd have to see what he could sniff out around the compound. Somebody would have something. In a place like this, somebody was bound to have something— anything. Black metal didn't exactly attract well-adjusted peo- ple. Hard drugs and corpsepaint were symptoms of the same disease.

There was no telling what time it was when he finally crawled out of bed, still in his clothes from the night before. Everything ached, pulsed sickly. The fluids in his body had turned to glue. He threw on his boots, left the cinderblock shack, and just kind of wandered around the compound, feeling like the living dead.

The sunlight was white and cool. It was much warmer than the day before and the snow had given way to slicks of mud. Only a few people were out, but no one he recognized. This place was filled with weirdos and skinheads. Other than Seph, it seemed like all the women here were nineteen and homely, wearing undercuts, shitloads of piercings in their faces. The men were mostly lumbering and humorless militants with shaved heads, neck tattoos, jacked teeth. Everyone wore baggy brown coats and old rubber boots that looked like they'd been donated, a bunch of Uncle Festers. It was like how he imagined old Soviet labor camps.

Smoke rose from the tin chimney on the kitchen's roof. A rusted-out and spray-painted 4x4 slowly dug its way down the main road away from the compound, occasionally spinning its chained wheels before grabbing hold of the cold earth. And then it was gone. In its place he heard the muffled thrash of a crusty blackened thrash band coming from the hall on the other side of the field and decided to go check it out. But first he wanted to see where Roland was.

He checked the kitchen. Then he went and looked in the barn—Roland wasn't there either, just animals, the smell of shit. He went out to the tree line and pissed in a high arc, something he hadn't done since he was a little kid. The wind blew his piss back all over his hands. Fucking Christ. A tight series of popping noises flapped in the wind from far off, gunshots. The shots were controlled, rhythmic, sounded like target practice deep in the woods. He wondered if Roland was there. The thought of Roland out in the woods with these people, with no one to look after him, filled Max with an inexplicable dread, or maybe it was jealousy. Who the fuck cared? He wasn't exactly in the habit of exploring his feelings.

He could see the hall from here, a massive and crumbling storage barn. Max wiped his hands on his pants, made his way over there, carefully watching where he stepped, drums like rolling thunder, the scraping of the guitars getting louder. The big sliding doors were pulled shut, so he went through the smaller door off to the side.

It was at least ten degrees warmer inside, but still cold. Banks of weak fluorescents buzzed in the ceiling and it took a few seconds for his eyes to adjust. The smell of stale beer and sweat was instant, as familiar as home.

There were three teenagers on the stage at the far end of the room. The lead singer screamed like he'd been set on fire, all the tendons in his neck pulled tight, face bright red. His sweat-soaked T-shirt hugged his wiry torso. They were jamming on an old Darkthrone tune, maybe "Transylvanian Hunger." Only their version of it sounded like shit—sloppy and amateurish, all howling feedback and crashing cymbals—the kind of noise that ate away at your brain, made it impossible to think. They took one look at Max coming their way and then fell apart, almost as if they were embarrassed to be caught playing. They were star-struck; he saw it in their glassy eyes. Might as well have been Fenriz himself.

There was a skull-splitting lash of feedback, followed by a low electric hum, the idiot guitarist suddenly remembering to mute his strings.

On the wall behind the stage hung a large blue flag—a coat of arms obviously, but nothing Max recognized—bearing a yellow broadsword flanked by two points, which formed a trident.

The singer just stood there looking sheepish while the guitarist moved back behind the kit. The drummer threw on a studded leather jacket, lit a cigarette, and crossed his arms. They were real tough guys, alright. All three of them had shaved their heads, weird tattoos scrawled on their hands and necks. Max leaned on the stage with both hands, did a kind of awkward finger roll that somehow sounded thunderous in the empty hall, and then caught sight of three pint cans of Staropramen ringed together near the drum kit. "Can I get one of those?" he asked, gesturing to the beer.

The singer's eyes were vacant—there was nothing there—that snarling and disaffected look that young punks practice in the mirror until they get it just right. He gave a quick nod, squatted down, and plucked one of the cans from its ring. Then he lobbed it over.

Max surprised even himself by catching it. He cracked it open. The beer had been out too long and it tasted like shit, somehow warm even though it was cold in the barn, but still he downed it greedily, actually made his eyes water.

"You guys practicing for the festival?" Max asked.

"I know who you are," the singer said. "*Henosis*—that's good shit."

Max finished the rest of the beer, crushed the can, and dropped it to the ground. He burped long and low, a hint of bile at the base of his throat. He was already feeling a little better, but it wasn't good enough. He eyed the remaining two cans.

"Yeah?" Max said. "What's your name?"

"Mark."

"What's the name of your band?"

He thought for a moment, maybe translating the name to English. "Corpsemasturbator."

Max laughed—actual genuine laughter. Jesus Christ, it made his face hurt. "That's good. You're gonna sell a lot of records with that name. Thank you for the beer, Mark." He waited just a moment. "Now let me get another one."

At first, the kid just looked at Max in disbelief, like he was kidding. But of course he wasn't kidding. He hadn't eaten since the day before. He was starving and he was sick and the beer made him feel better. More beer would make him feel even better. Right now he could afford to feel much better. If they wouldn't give him what he wanted—what he needed—then he'd take it. He'd take what he could get, not just because he could, but because it was what he was owed for being made to suffer.

Mark got the message. Maybe he wasn't as stupid as he looked. He was eager to please, pulled another beer from the ring. This time he walked over and extended his arm, handed it to Max. And that was when Max saw the track marks along the inside of the kid's elbow, just beneath the sleeve of his shirt, the tight grouping of red puncture wounds, the brownish yellow bruising. Max took the beer, closed his eyes as he poured it down his throat.

He felt euphoric. It was so easy sometimes, like an energy source that draws upon surrounding bodies, feeds off of them and becomes stronger. You wake up and you need something and you go outside and there it is, just waiting for you.

"Do your friends speak English?" Max said.

Mark shook his head. "No."

"But you do?"

"Yes." The kid waited a second. "I went to my classes at school."

"In that case I'll just talk to you." He took another long sip of the beer. "I heard you guys playing. You're pretty good. Are you signed?"

Mark's whole demeanor suddenly changed. He dropped the tough guy act. "We've had some interest," he said, which was a bald-faced lie. "We're about to go on our first tour."

"Listen," Max said, "I'm here to work on an album. You know that, right? My label is looking for new talent, asked me to send them some leads. You guys have a lot of potential. You got a demo?"

The kid actually licked his lips, he was so eager. "Hell yeah we do. We've got about fifteen minutes of stuff that we've put down. I can get you a tape." He got down on his knees and started digging around in a backpack at his feet, barking out a few terse statements to his bandmates in their native language. The guitarist forgot he was muting the strings for a second, pointing at something. There was another lash of ear-shredding feedback from the guitar, sounding like a scream. Then the feedback cut, Max's ears ringing. His face must have given away how irritated he was because the kid actually apologized in terrible English, face red. God, his fucking headache. Then Mark was back, handing Max a cassette in a hard plastic case. The band logo was indecipherable, scrawled in black marker.

Max put the cassette in his pocket. He pointed at the kid's guitar. "You mind if I play a little?" He killed the rest of the beer and got up on the stage, sat down on the amp. The guitarist quickly handed Max the SG. It felt good in his hands, felt just right.

He looked around the stage, all the shit just lying around, all beat-up and junky. There was a Peavey PXD Tomb with broken pickups and a ridiculous Ibanez seven-string with ornate silver dragons on the frets. The only acoustic had a cracked nut and a warped neck. The stacks looked like they'd been stomped with steel-toed boots, buried beneath layer upon layer of half-peeled stickers for forgotten punk and metal bands. The pedals were ancient but they were classics, a Tube Screamer, a Boss HM-2. And then there was the drum kit—totally beat to shit.

"You like my early stuff, right?" He launched into the riff from one of his most recognizable songs, "Labyrinth Architect," an intricate little thing that had to be played lightning fast, all interlocking parts and furious shredding.

They were in awe, all three of them. Max relished moments like this. He'd always been a gifted guitarist—the instrument came naturally to him—even when he was sick, he could still slay. After a while he played a few other riffs, all from his first three albums, gave the kids what they wanted to hear. He showed them a better way to do "Transylvanian Hunger." And when he was done, he turned off the amp and looked Mark in the eye. The kid was giddy. He'd be telling his friends about this moment for the rest of his life.

Max had him exactly where he wanted him.

"I'm happy to send along your tape," he said, "but I was wondering if you could do something for me in return. I couldn't help but notice the marks on your arm. They're fresh. Don't be embarrassed. Listen, can you hook me up with some of your shit?"

The smile was long gone from Mark's face. He looked worried. He absentmindedly ran his fingers over the bruises on his inner arm.

Of all the drugs to ask someone for, heroin was the least cool. Ask anyone for weed or coke or meth and everything was hunky-dory, but as soon as you mention smack, it was like you'd outed yourself as a death freak—even between two users. It didn't matter.

Of course there was Agnes's warning—that Seph didn't like people on the compound using. There were rules against it. Wisdom had supposedly murdered their drummer because he'd been running drugs. Falchik. These kids were worried that Seph would find out they were junkies. Not like they were doing a good job hiding the evidence… Or maybe they were connected to Falchik in some way. Either way, he wasn't sure what it was, but they were scared. And their fear gave Max the leverage he needed.

Everyone had a weakness. Power was simply a matter of identifying that weakness, figuring out how to pull it open like a freshly healed wound and stick your finger in.

"You know," he said, "I've heard rumors about this place—

maybe you can tell me if they're crazy or not. A friend of mine told me that a guy was murdered here. His name was Falchik. She said he sold drugs. You know anything about that?"

Mark's bandmates may not have spoken English, but they definitely recognized the name of Wisdom's drummer. The guitar player said something in Ukrainian and then spit on the stage, staring levelly at Max.

"What did he just say?" Max asked.

"That your questions will get you killed," Mark said.

"Oh, yeah?"

Mark nodded, his lips pursed. He was starting to get mad. That was good. Anger made people impulsive.

"Listen," Max said, "I'm not trying to get you in trouble. I don't care what you do. I'm American. I think everyone should be free to do whatever the fuck they want. All I want from you is a hookup. You help me out and I help you out and everything stays quiet."

"But that's not—"

"Fuck it," Max said, his slow-rising frustration finally bubbling over. "I thought you guys would be cool." He took the cassette out of his pocket and tried to give it back to Mark. "You've got other interest in your demo, at least."

Mark stared at the tape in Max's hand, thinking it over. He turned to the others and the three of them exchanged a few tense words in their native language. Max didn't give a shit what they were saying. It didn't matter. He reached down and picked up the third and last can of beer, popped it open. It was his now, was even starting to taste better.

In the time it took them to talk through whatever it was they needed to talk through, he finished the beer. And when Mark turned around, Max already knew what he was going to say.

4

Roland held the AK-47 with the stock nestled against his shoulder, just like Seph had shown him. He pulled back the switch, the sound of it, the deathly precision of the thing in his hands, utterly cold and clinical. He eyed the nearest target, a black paper bullseye tacked to a bale of hay, some ten or twenty yards away. Then he curled his finger around the trigger and squeezed—immediately letting go. The gun erupted with a controlled fury, doing its best to jump out of his hands. He squeezed the trigger again, let go. Again, let go. His shots went wild. The first one ripped into the ground nowhere near the target and the second shattered part of the woodpile at the edge of the clearing. The third shot didn't seem to land anywhere at all.

He carefully laid the gun on the lip of an empty oil drum and pulled off his ear protection. Sound flooded in—the winter wind, the whisperings of dead trees. Seph came to him smiling, her platinum hair pulled into a high ponytail, exposing the shaved sides of her head. She wore leather boots, a baggy camo jacket, tight black jeans—a fashion model playing soldier. He couldn't understand what she was doing out here. She didn't belong here. She belonged on billboards with that smile. She belonged in magazine ads.

"You're getting better," Seph said, picking up the gun, barrel still smoking. She ejected the magazine, the routine of it automatic and unthinking. "Don't be afraid to scare yourself." She snapped a fresh magazine into place. Her boots groaned as she pivoted and dropped to one knee. Roland heard the metallic crunch of the switch, had just enough time to clap his hands over his ears before Seph unloaded thirty rounds. Then she was up on her feet, knees bent slightly, swift movement. She ejected the empty magazine and loaded another, firing into the target to her left, the target to her right. The sound of the cracking gunshots massed into a swirling cloud, echoing enormously through the empty gray sky.

It was the sound of Seattle rainstorms rumbling behind broken glass. Roland recalled so many endless nights spent freebasing meth by candlelight in vacant, crumbling buildings, the smell of mildew, the chill of cold brick. When you live like that, you learn firsthand the need to protect yourself. Every sound in the dark signals a threat. You get used to the electric jolt of adrenaline in your bloodstream—even as you sleep. And after a while you don't even notice the weight of the knife tucked away in your boot. It's how you survive.

He knew then, as he watched Seph burn through magazine after magazine, that this was how she had learned to survive. She didn't belong on billboards, nothing more than an image selling a fantasy. No, images were harmless.

Later, as they made their way back to the compound, Seph talked at length about how to approach an unknown area and take control, how to focus a line of sight through an open window and slice the pie, carefully strafing, only claiming amounts of ground that you know are safe—until you can see and therefore eliminate the target.

"You seem to spend a lot of time thinking about how to kill people," Roland said, the words escaping his lips before he thought to stop them. Fuck it. His ears were still ringing and his nerves felt raw. Firing the rifle had upset something in him, shaken something loose, the unpleasant taste of guilt in his mouth. But what? He thought of the knife he'd left back in Seattle, stashed in a coin locker at the YMCA along with everything else he couldn't fit in his duffel bag, all the stuff he couldn't bring on the plane. It wasn't much, a stack of old photographs, some papers, road maps, a Zippo lighter that had once belonged to his dad. They were things he wouldn't miss, things he didn't need anymore. At least that's what he'd told himself, that if he were somehow able to start a new life somewhere—maybe in Chicago, maybe overseas—that he would never need those things again. Maybe that was it. And maybe firing the gun, his mind returning once more to thoughts of survival, of killing, had brought back the fear he'd worked so hard to leave behind.

"All men hold murder in their hearts," Seph said. She looked levelly at Roland until he looked away, an annoying habit of hers. She was always so intense. "You wish people dead a hundred times each day without a second thought, for even the slightest offenses. Someone takes your seat on a crowded bus. Someone cuts you off in traffic, blows their smoke in your face. You wish them dead. Everyone does this. Imagine how utterly decimated the human race would be if each of those wishes had come true."

Roland tracked the flight of a black bird with long tail feathers, a stagnant shadow gliding over the rippled surface of the sky. It looked fake, superimposed. They were maybe a hundred yards out from the compound. From here it looked like little more than smoking heaps of scrap, a mess fit to be razed.

"People think like that because it's harmless," he said. "Thinking murderous thoughts never killed anyone."

"You think so? Maybe the reason people like me spend so much time thinking about killing people, is that when we have to do it, we're ready to do it."

He let this sink in. "So you've killed someone?"

Seph looked off into the distance, recalling something, seeing something replay in her memory. She carried the AK in a black bag strapped over her shoulder. She switched the bag from one shoulder to the other. "Not in the way you might think."

He couldn't even begin to understand what that meant, didn't care to. All he wanted to do was write music, play the guitar, bang on some drums. It had been more than a week since he'd so much as held a pair of sticks. And finally, today, he thought he'd get to practice. But some other band had been using the hall that morning, talentless shitheads. So he'd gone to Seph to ask how to reserve practice time and instead of helping him she'd dragged him out to the clearing in the woods. You've never fired a gun before? Feigning surprise. Then you have no idea how good it feels. I promise you it will help with creativity, release your pent-up energy.

It will help with the music, she said. Trust me.

He'd trusted her. Even now he could feel the gun's awful vibrations in the bones of his hands—the way each shot sent a shudder through his teeth.

Roland felt more trapped than ever before, claustrophobic, despite the limitlessness of the surrounding landscape. Whatever had shaken loose had left emptiness in its place, and that emptiness had soon filled with a confusion of voices.

"Are you OK?" she asked.

"I'm just tired. Shooting guns and talking about killing people makes me feel tired."

She dropped the gun bag to the ground and just stood there, arms crossed.

Roland took a few more steps before he realized she'd fallen behind. He turned and faced her. She wore no makeup, though her cheeks were flushed red. His heart was suddenly in his throat. He'd danced around it in his mind all this time but now he knew that he was scared of her because she was beautiful. Or, he wasn't scared of her as much as he was scared of being attracted to her, because surely no good could come of such a thing. He wasn't in her league.

"It's quite the luxury to feel tired by confronting violence," she said.

"That's not what I—"

"Did you know that Moscow tells the people of Ukraine that their country is run by radicals and terrorists? No? They spread misinformation, fear. They convince the *ovets* in the east and in the south to give up defending their own country. And these people, they stop speaking their native language. In Kiev they teach their children Russian in the schools."

Roland shrugged. "So what?"

"So why do you think I live out here?"

"Because you don't like other people telling you what to do."

"It's more than that," she said. "I live out here because I believe it will better allow me to defend my country when the time comes. I live out here because it allows me to be free from oppression. The people in the cities are enslaved by false religions, by Islam and by Christianity. But we live as free people, as people were intended to live. I can see from your face that you don't understand why I'm telling you this. I want you to understand what this place is. It's important that you understand. I see something in you—a similarity, perhaps." She stepped forward and put her hand on his arm, looking up into his eyes. "I saw it when you first arrived. You've been running away your whole life and now you've finally come to a place where you belong."

Roland thought he might throw up. She stood so close to him that he could see the pores in her skin. She was much smaller than him. He hadn't noticed until just now that her teeth were also small. They were yellow and too close together. This somehow made her even more beautiful. "I'm not sure your friend Grigore would agree with that."

"Why?" Her forehead creased. "Did he say something to you?"

"He didn't have to."

Seph laughed nervously. Her hand fell away from Roland's arm. "He is wary of all outsiders, but he is no threat. He's protective. It's just who he is." She leaned down and retrieved the gun bag, slung it over her shoulder once more. "I don't mean to lecture you. You are here now and you are going to have to learn to trust us."

It was as if he had imagined the whole thing, as if nothing had happened. It was easier than thinking about it. They walked the rest of the way in silence.

Seph unlocked the door of one of the metal sheds on the outskirts of the compound. Inside, Roland saw the rigid outlines of steel shelves gleaming in the dark, ammo cases along the floor, rifle racks and unidentifiable piles of equipment and machinery. She tossed the heavy black bag onto a low shelf and then pulled the door shut, secured the lock. "We believe that a person should die in an act of aggression," she said. "All other deaths lack nobility."

It was a weird thing to say.

Roland was just about to respond when he heard the heavy rumble of a diesel engine behind him. He looked over his shoulder and saw a black 4x4 tearing down the main road toward the compound, the wall of oily exhaust in its wake nearly obscuring the white van that followed.

"There's your friend now," Seph said jokingly. Or at least it sounded like a joke, an attempt to cover up the fact that maybe Seph was worried about Grigore, too. She'd been so quick to ask if he'd said anything, and that crease in her forehead was well worn.

The 4x4 pulled alongside them, slowly rolling through the mud, the chains on its tires biting into the half-frozen ground. The driver's side window was down. Pounding black metal poured from the speakers, sounding like a waterfall, all rushing treble and hiss. Grigore wore mirror shades, leaned with his arm out the window like a long-haul trucker. He said something in Ukrainian to Seph, gestured to the van behind him. Seph nodded, said *dobre*, a word Roland was beginning to recognize in regular conversation. The two of them exchanged a few sentences. Then Grigore looked Roland's way, smiled a knowing smile. There was nothing friendly in that smile. Roland didn't give a shit what Seph said—the guy was a threat. And even though his eyes were hidden behind shades, Roland knew Grigore was glaring at him.

The big diesel engine snarled to life and the 4x4 pulled away, grinding through the mud, music fading into the distance. The van quickly followed. Roland recognized it as the van from the day before—the one Grigore had used to pick him and Max up at the airport. It was starting to look like that hike through the woods had been some kind of test, maybe even a trial. He couldn't help but wonder what else around here was not quite what it seemed.

5

Over the next few days, the young black goat quickly found his strength. He was deformed, the little monster, with legs much shorter than usual, gnarled with twisted bones, and only one of his coal-gleamed eyes opened, the other a twisted flap of skin sealed tight. The result was an uneven pull on his mouth, which gave the impression of a crooked smile, a knowing smirk.

Taras named the kid Likho, after the one-eyed demon of evil and misfortune. He certainly lived up to his name, always off chasing shadows, escaping his pen, bounding about recklessly. Once, he nearly set the barn on fire after kicking over a thoughtlessly placed heat lamp. Hecate, for whatever reason, refused to nurse him, choosing instead to butt or kick him whenever he drew close. Even offerings of fresh grain would not change her mind.

Or maybe Hecate was able to intuit that something else was wrong, the certain smell of death in the air. The old nanny was the first animal in the barn to come down with what appeared to be flu-like symptoms. Seph found her one morning in her pen, on her side, taking shallow breaths, eyes glazed over. The flies had already claimed her as their own, swarming her open mouth, her unblinking eyes. Hecate's legs were caked with diarrhea and a thick yellow discharge oozed from her glistening nose. It was most likely Leptospirosis, or maybe even Q fever, and the major concern was keeping the illness from spreading to the other animals. Of course, there was nowhere to move the other animals—they only had the one barn—and it was too cold to set up pens outdoors. Diseases like this spread quickly, even to humans. They were left with no choice but to put the old nanny out of her misery, a task Seph assigned to Taras, who did not mind such unpalatable work. He even seemed to welcome it, claiming that a mercy killing, an offering of a mother goat, however aged, would please the Lord.

Despite Hecate's illness, and the subsequent worry she harbored for the well-being of the other animals, Seph felt renewed. There was no use in fighting the will of nature. It had always been this way: from death came life, a new sense of optimism. And for Seph, this optimism blossomed from her spending more time with the drummer.

They were alike in some ways, teenage runaways drawn to music, lovers of art. And in other ways, they were different. He lacked strong convictions, self-confidence. But he was an attentive listener, thoughtful, and able to articulate his musical ideas with remarkable clarity. They talked for hours, over tea, on walks, sitting across from one another at the long table. He talked at great length about paintings that he loved and she did her best to explain her Ukrainian heritage. He never treated her as anything other than an equal. She'd never expected any real feelings to develop, at least not at first, but then something changed. He inspired her, ignited something long dormant, a passion to create—she even began to conceive of new material for Wisdom—and this was where their connection developed into something more.

Nearly a week passed before they slept together. He was so

passive that she had to literally invite him back to her room late one night.

They stood face to face in the darkness of her room. She commanded him to undress. His upper arms, chest, and thighs were neatly laddered with self-inflicted scars. She ran her fingers over the raised tissue, pale, smooth to the touch. She kissed his face, his chest. He kept his eyes shut, an almost pained expression on his face, breathing loudly through his nose. She asked him if he was alright, if this was OK, if he needed more time. He said yes, that he was fine, he was ready.

The first time they had sex, Seph had to do all of the work, which suited her well enough. He was not a great kisser, his skin was clammy, and his hands shook. He needed to learn to let go—to scare himself. She used her own saliva to make it easier for him and when he entered her she thought of Grigore. She thought of how many times she had fucked or been fucked and only because the man demanded it, only because it was what two people were supposed to do, something to do to pass the time. She opened her legs wider for him and suddenly he kissed her deeply, asserted himself. She knew him then. It was over in just a few minutes.

Fucking brought them closer. Seph found that afterward, perhaps surprisingly, she did not want to kick him out of her bed. They talked until the sun came up, sharing cigarettes, laughing goofily, teaching each other new words.

Where had Grigore gone? He was giving her space, spending nights off the compound, doing fuck-all probably. She thought of things she could wrap her head around, things that added up to something real. The money they had received from Strigoi's record label was starting to run low—and this was going to be a long winter. Temperatures continued to drop. An ice storm came and went, knocking out the electricity. The repairs were costly, time consuming. Irena had split, probably hitting the road with one of the bands that used the hall. Even with Dusanka pulling double-duty, handling both the cooking and the cleaning, Seph's responsibilities had still increased. She resolved to keep a closer eye on things. She needed to exert more control, keep a tighter grip on things.

She'd lost control once before, years ago, gotten distracted. And look what had happened. Falchik had flooded the compound with Afghani opium and Russian heroin. Late in the summer they found the decomposed corpses of a young man and woman in one of the trailers out in the field, both of them valued workers. That had been the end of that.

She held Roland tight as he slept next to her, together in her bed, breathing in the smell of him, a smell that was now somewhat familiar, perhaps now more like her own. And in this moment she began to believe that maybe she could trust him, that maybe he would understand her way of life, her beliefs.

There was always more work to do. And there would always be more work to do. As much as she hated to admit it, Wisdom's music had always taken a backseat to the work, always would. The real work was here, this place. They had to begin preparations for the Winter Solstice festival, which started in a few days. They needed to set up equipment for nearly a dozen bands, prepare enough food for a hundred people. It was going to be difficult, but they needed the money it would bring in now more than ever, now that so many people relied on her, on the compound. And for this she was thankful for the Americans. Their presence had done much to raise awareness of the festival, everyone hoping to catch a glimpse of the famous Strigoi.

If she was unable to focus on her music, at least Roland could focus on his. That's what was important. Once Strigoi's album was finished they would receive the rest of the money from his label. He had to keep working. Depending on how long he stayed here, how much food he ate, how much electricity he used, how much time he spent consuming their resources, he might even still be owed something for his efforts.

6

They got to work. Max got together with Roland in the hall each morning or afternoon or whatever it was, it didn't matter, and Roland would riff on the drums. He was like a brainless idiot when he got behind the kit, capable of laying down 290 beats per minute, tight fills, never slipping up. He was a machine. Max would come in with his guitar and they'd vary what they were playing every few bars, waiting to see what clicked. Not much did click, but the sound was there, out-of-tune, ruinous white heat.

It was the kind of sound that conjured images of decay and neglect. Most of the lower frets on the guitar he used were gunked with finger grease, dried blood, or so Max liked to imagine. Lead lines would rupture with feedback and chords sounded shambolic, notes repellant, pulling away from one another. He refused to accept that a thing in all its elements should have to behave otherwise, governed by an inner pull, oppressed by the gravity of its center.

This sound was everything he'd tried so hard to find for so long, killed himself for, gone into debt for, hiring expensive engineers, dicking around in expensive studios, only to find it out here in this frozen and forsaken place where people lived on nothing but vegetables and hot water like peasants in an old Russian novel.

He had to admit that the kid was more than good, probably the best he'd ever played with, if he was being honest. Not that he'd ever tell him that. A thing like that goes straight to a person's head and, like the rest of him, the kid's head was already big enough.

But everything was fucked. No matter how much they played, they just couldn't synch up. The ideas weren't there—only the noise. Max was always going off about his ideas, complex structures and weird time signatures that Roland couldn't wrap his head around. Let's try this, let's play it like this. But it was like Max could never explain his ideas in a way that Roland understood. When Roland talked about his ideas Max could only hear a bunch of spacey bullshit. It was like they spoke different languages entirely. The music was the one thing that could hold Max together and it was falling apart. Frustration turned to anger. And when Max got pissed at the kid, when they got pissed off at each other, which happened sooner and with more intensity each time they got together, they'd call it a day and head their separate ways.

Each session was a slow deterioration, a creeping image of a car crash, the odd angles of shattered glass suspended in time and catching the light like stars. Each time Max went off on his own, each time he dipped into his dwindling supply of black tar, he felt that there was that much less holding him together.

He spent long nights in the hall by himself, fucked up on drugs, messing around with different instruments, totally aimless, lost. He'd nearly burned through the shit Mark had given him. It was low grade, probably cut with something heavy, animal tranq or maybe even something even worse. He didn't want to think about it. The risk of an overdose was better than the sickness creeping. Not that he could hold it off forever. He was going to run out soon.

And then he did. And then he got sick. And then he went crazy.

The day of the festival arrived and it was like the circus coming to town. There were half a dozen vans, trucks, a couple RVs, everyone unloading equipment, people everywhere. Max watched from the window of his concrete shack, too sick, too fucking crazy to go out and show his face. Besides, Mark knew where to find him, right? He waited for Mark to find him. Mark was supposed to drop off more shit before his set—he'd promised.

There was no telling how long Max waited. He waited until it was dark outside, until his stomach felt hard and twisted, his tongue glued to the roof his mouth. And then he waited even longer. Still Mark did not arrive.

Night fell. The festival kicked off, the sound of drums rolling and guitars chugging, a feeling of energy crackling through the air.

But here in his room, Max couldn't hear any of that, only the mechanical hiss of the space heater. The thing was fucking useless. Even with the heater cranked on full blast, the metal grill glowing bright red, he was still freezing cold. Didn't matter that he was sweating through his shirt, he was fucking freezing. He lay down and shut his eyes, freakish visions unspooling in the dark. He saw them take Roland away. All dressed in black like a crazy cult, they took him out into the woods, chained him to an ancient and black-barked tree, and tore him open. A splash of steaming black blood fanned out against the white snow, a metallic smell attracting great unseen beasts, shrouded in outlying darkness, the bellow of hot breath beyond the tree line. He heard their calls not nearly far enough away and came screaming awake.

His stomach cramped with cold. He was an alien in human

skin. The thought of it—the horror of getting sick again—brought burning tears to his eyes. He'd promised himself this would never happen again. He was always letting himself down. And now they'd taken Roland away from him and left him all alone.

That was just a dream, though. Had that really been a dream?

Max went outside, the awful sound of music suddenly everywhere, and made it ten steps before his feet slipped out from beneath him. The sky turned overhead at an angle and stars burst into slow-drifting tinsel when his head smacked against the ice. He opened his eyes in a black void, somehow filled with the knowledge that he was awake and calm at the bottom of a black sea, stagnant gray sands as far as he could see. And there in the distance, a great spire, a beacon of light. There was no pain in this place, no sickness, only relief. He let the relief wash over him. The world beyond the black sea hummed deep and mysterious. But then the still waters filled with a searing light, as if the light of the beacon found him. He felt himself lifted toward the light-rippled surface, weightless, the immense image of a stretched and bloated man's face blotting out the sky, warped from strange undulations. The skin on the bloated man's face was crawling with wretched and broken figures. His skin was alive.

Suddenly Max was awake again and on his feet, searching.

He wasn't sure what he was looking for. He wasn't sure where to find it. He pushed through groups of faceless people, everyone staring.

And then he pushed through the door to the warm kitchen. The whole place went silent. He sat down at the end of the long table. When he realized that no one was going to ask him if he needed anything he slammed his hand against the table as hard as he could, his knuckles ringing with sound. He tasted blood. He saw the bloated man's face when he closed his eyes, skin shuddering with awful movement. Mother of God. He needed a drink. The girl in the apron who was always chopping vegetables peeked out from behind a large and steaming pot. She came over and stood there, leaning too close, looking at Max like his face held some secret, like she was reading his soul. Her mouth moved but he couldn't understand a word she said and when she got closer than too close he reached out and stretched his hand wide across her face, shoving her away. She was lighter than he'd ever imagined a person could be—the weight of a small child, if that—and she fell backward onto the floor, crying out. The sound of her surprise was like a siren in Max's scrambled brain, cutting through the gunk and fog. He was suddenly aware of the shapes of men in his periphery. There were two of them, dressed in black, and they were closing in on him. Were these the men who had taken Roland away? One loomed behind, over his shoulder, waiting, and the other before him, watching. This one, the watcher, looked so much like Roman. But he was actually an alien in human skin.

The one who looked like Roman helped the girl to her feet. She was scared, crying, lower lip trembling, and it made her look ugly. She pushed away, covered her face with her arm and pushed through the door outside, vanishing.

Roman spoke to Max but Max couldn't understand a word he said. It was all scrambled.

"I need a drink," Max said, maybe louder than intended. "Vodka."

Then it was like Roman's language came together, words like drops of mercury globbing together, forming whole. "You're bleeding," he said, speaking slowly. "What happened?"

A small glass appeared on the table in front of Max. Roman held a bottle by its neck, turned it sideways. He filled the glass with a clear liquid. Then he set the bottle on the table, out of reach. Max picked up the glass and drank it immediately and all at once. The vodka stripped his throat, utterly corrosive, homemade shit. Good shit. He smacked the cup against the table.

"Another," Max said.

"I am not sure that's a good idea," Roman said.

He heard the voice of the other, the one who stood behind him, the one who waited. "Are you in pain? Can you tell us what happened to you?"

Of course he was in pain. What kind of question was that? Every waking moment was pain. He was being ripped apart from the inside. He'd woken up that morning and someone had turned him inside out. He was all twitching, dying nerves and soft pink tissue exposed in the light, glistening and throbbing. He wanted nothing more than to take his pain and transfer it onto another, to rid himself of his burden. Maybe he would show one of these men who wore black what kind of pain he was feeling. Maybe he would let them know.

"I really would like another drink, please."

His voice sounded so hurt, was so pathetic, that it made him want to cry.

"You are hurt," Roman said. Now he searched Max's face just as the girl had, as if it held a secret. Why wouldn't they just tell him what was written in the blood on his face? "You may have concussion. Alcohol is not the best thing for concussion."

Fuck it. Max leaned forward and grabbed the bottle, got his hand around it. But Roman was fast, much faster than Max, and ripped the bottle away. It happened so fast. And then it was like a great gulf cracked open between that moment and whatever the next moment might be. Terror flooded into this gulf. Max sensed that the one behind him, the one who waited, would soon wrap an arm around his neck, could almost feel it. The fear of being restrained jolted through his whole body. He jumped to his feet, slid around Roman, who instinctively cradled the bottle in his arm against his chest, turning away. But Max wasn't going for the bottle—he didn't give a fuck about the bottle anymore—now he was trying to get away. These men were going to kill him just like they'd killed Roland. Only he'd gone the wrong way, away from the door that led outside. He'd gone deeper into the room, near the counter. He heard the boil of the steaming pot, the hiss of the gas range, felt its heat radiating, the smell of soil. Now he was trapped. The two of them—the men who wore black, the waiter and the watcher—had him cornered.

How had he gotten here? He couldn't remember.

The door to the world outside opened and closed. The crying child with the ugly face was back, and she'd brought others, people Max didn't recognize. The girl screamed, pointing at Max, screamed again, her words scrambled in the alien tongue. Roman and the other one both turned to her, distracted. Without thinking about what it was or why, Max grabbed whatever it was on the counter, an object gleaming in the light, something he could use to defend himself, something that felt heavy in his hand—a butcher knife. He swung the knife from side to side and his attackers backed away. They were giving him space, allowing him an escape. He didn't think about it, just took off running through the doorway and into the night, a swarm of menacing and buzzing voices calling out to him to stop.

7

The pit was dark, blaring stage lights unable to penetrate the dense crowd. Roland stomped through the writhing mass, double-bass pounding, guitars churning. The heavyset tattooed guy onstage let loose a death growl, barking out incomprehensible lyrics, and the band summoned wave after wave of sternum-pummeling noise. A beer bottle arced overhead, turning end over end. Roland took an elbow to the ribs, grabbed the back of some skinny kid's sweaty neck and threw him spinning to the ground where he was stomped and kicked until he disappeared, eaten alive by the tangled mass. Someone's knee connected with Roland's thigh. He gritted his teeth, shoved people out of his way. It was the most fun he'd had since God knew when, just letting loose and being in the moment. The band started grinding in triple time and the crowd went absolutely nuts, dissonant guitars scraping, everyone in the crowd and on the stage banging their heads in unison.

There was a triple bill that night. A hippie-looking doom band with an unpronounceable Ukrainian name was up next, then a crusty black-metal band with a stupid name—Corpsemasturbator. If all the bands were as good as these guys, it was going to be an awesome evening.

A hand came down hard on Roland's shoulder, spun him around, nearly threw him off balance. It was Grigore, looking pissed—looking for a fight. Roland was charged up. He knew in that moment that he was ready for this, that somewhere in the recesses of his mind he'd been preparing for this. He shoved Grigore hard in the chest with both hands, but it was like pushing against a brick wall. Grigore's top lip pulled back. He grabbed the collar of Roland's shirt and pulled him in close so they were face to face, their feet fumbling in an awkward dance. "This is how it is?" Grigore yelled. Roland couldn't hear shit, felt Grigore's hot breath on his cheek. And then Grigore barked something else into his ear, pointed to the back of the room. The crowd surged and almost pulled Roland along with it but Grigore held on, pointing again, with more emphasis this time. Roland could just barely make out Seph along the back wall of the room, waving her arm over her head, trying to get his attention.

He made his way toward her, following close behind Grigore, who threw people out of the way like they were nothing, adrenaline still racing. He caught a glimpse of Seph as she slipped out the door. Something was up.

Night had fallen and the sweat on Roland's skin steamed in the cool air. They found Seph near one of the work sheds. Max was somewhere on the compound, she explained, and he was injured, likely confused. She spoke quickly, handed out flashlights. He needed to be found before he hurt someone else or himself. "No violence," she said, staring at Grigore.

Whatever fun Roland was having at the show was now a distant memory, illusory, weirdly tinged with guilt. What the fuck was Max's problem? As he followed the trail of boot prints in the cracked and broken snow, the worryingly frequent spatterings of blood, Roland thought back to that freezing morning in Chicago, seemingly a lifetime ago, when he'd shouldered a dazed and bleeding Max out of the projects. Nothing had changed since then; he was painfully aware of that now. Max was hellbent on self-destruction—that was his problem. What did you do with a person like that? You had to let them go, that's what. There was no helping a person like that. People like that don't want to be helped. It was that simple.

Yet here he was, chasing after the selfish bastard once more, tracking blood in the snow like a hunter pursuing wounded prey. The honest truth was that he wasn't sure he cared if he found Max or not, wasn't sure he cared if he was alive or dead. More than anything he was annoyed that the responsibility was at least partly his.

"Somebody should have followed him," he said.

Grigore laughed. Roland turned and glared, kept trudging forward.

"We've gone over this," Seph said. "Dusanka was hysterical. Roman and the others remained to calm her down." She paused, shook her head. "People are already talking about how the famous Strigoi has lived up to his reputation as a madman. Pictures of him will be all over the Internet in just a few days."

They didn't know the half of it. Roland had seen firsthand the way Max could slip behind a veil of darkness, disappearing into another version of himself, prone to violent outbursts, totally unpredictable. Or maybe that was the real Max, the maniac, the one withdrawn from the world inhabited by others, governed by laws. He could only imagine how frightening it must have been for Dusanka, someone who didn't know Max for shit. All she'd done was gone over to see if he was hurt. And Max had slapped her across the mouth.

"Why would he attack her?" Seph asked.

"He's a sick fuck," Grigore said. "That's why."

Roland ignored him. "He's fucked up," he said. "Some days he can barely play the guitar, forgets things. His hands shake.

Then he gets mad and accuses me of playing too fast, says I'm trying to fuck him up on purpose, blames me for not being able to keep time. He needs our help."

The sessions had been going poorly, Seph knew this. Each night before bed Roland poured out his frustrations, vented his anger. Working with the so-called tortured genius was a total drag. No wonder he'd burned through so many hired guns over the years. He was impossible.

They climbed a rotting wood fence and hopped over the dip of the half-frozen irrigation canal, entering one of the endless flat fields beyond the compound. The music from the show was barely audible from this distance, only the muffled thumps of the bass drum skipping along. It was dark, dreary gray, the moon obscured by clouds.

A few moments later they approached the crumbling, snow-covered camper trailers. Seph shined her light on the nearest one, its narrow windows busted out, paint chipped, thin scraps of metal trim bent at odd angles. There were rust-lined creases in the flimsy metal door, as if someone had long ago tried to kick it in. She tried the handle but it wouldn't budge.

Roland brushed an inch or two of powdery snow from the trailer hitch on one of the campers. It was completely rusted through, probably left rotting for years.

"He's been here," he said, speaking quietly. "Look at the tracks."

Seph swung the beam of her flashlight; it webbed wide against the silver-streaked body of an ancient, derelict RV. There were streaks of dried blood all around the handle. And even though the surrounding snow was deep enough that the tires of the RV were half-buried, a large patch of it in front of the RV's door was packed down flat, as if Max had been coming and going regularly.

Grigore cradled his flashlight beneath his arm. He reached behind and under his jacket and pulled free a jet-black handgun, chambered a bullet. The sound of it was sharp as an ice pick.

"What the fuck is that for?" Roland said, keeping his voice low. He shined his light on Grigore, who instinctively held a large hand up before his face. Grigore's flashlight dropped away from beneath his arm and bit into the snow, its beam angled up into the sky.

"Get your light out of my face," Grigore said, almost hissing. He swore in Ukrainian, quickly bent down and retrieved the flashlight.

The two of them stood glaring at each other.

Seph turned and held a single finger before her lips, looking furious and resentful at the same time, as if she were scolding misbehaving children. Then she climbed up onto the metal stairs and peeked in through the fogged porthole window. She pulled on the handle and popped open the door, slipped inside. Roland followed, feeling the need to put himself between Max and Grigore. He worried about the gun. No, that wasn't quite right. He worried about Grigore.

The window curtains were all pulled and the inside of the RV was dark, somehow even colder than it was outside. Seph quickly made her way to the sleeper cabin in the back, calling out Max's name, asking if he was OK, checking various compartments along the way, slamming them shut. The beams of light illumined the cramped interior space a bright, icy blue, accentuated a milky coating of grime on the walls and tabletops. Roland felt the crunch of garbage beneath his feet, empty cans and junk-food bags. He toed an empty wine bottle into a sharp corner where it shattered, and cursed under his breath. The air smelled like rotting pumpkins. There were cigarette butts everywhere, ruined spider webs drifting along the ceiling.

Seph emerged from the shadows of the RV's sleeper cabin. "He's not here," she said, "but he's been here. There's needles and shit back there."

"Needles?" Grigore said.

Seph nodded. "He's been using this place as a shooting gallery." She gave Roland an inquisitive look, raising her eyebrows.

"Don't look at me," he said. "He's always fucked up—no more fucked up than usual."

"If he's not here, then where is he?" Grigore said. "We followed his tracks."

"We must have missed something," Seph said. "He doubled back or went around the far edge of the field, used the canal to hide his tracks. I don't know."

"He's not that smart," Roland said.

Seph exhaled loudly, frustrated. "We'll come back tomorrow to clean this place out. For now, we should head back. We need to find him."

Much later, after things had settled like so much dust, Roland wondered what would have happened if they hadn't gone all the way out to the camper trailers, wasted all of that time. What if they'd waited another half hour, run into Max before he'd gotten to the hall? Or better yet, what if Roland had been with Max earlier in the day? It was stupid to think that way, to wonder what might have been, he knew that, but he couldn't stop it. There was no other way to make sense of it all. And he did struggle to make sense of it all, wanted so badly to believe that things could have been different, would have given anything to make things right.

They passed several bonfires as they returned to the compound, a group of shirtless metalheads wrestling in the snow, barking at one another like junkyard dogs. The festival had kicked into high gear. A menacing cloud of smoke had settled over everything, smelling like diesel.

Roman was waiting for them, pacing before the entrance to the hall. "Max is here," he said. "He was a mess. Covered in blood. All the kids are trying to buy him drinks. They think it's his act. He said he wanted to go back to the green room and lie down, so I took him there."

They didn't waste any time. Seph led the way, pushed through the swaying crowd. The next band had taken the stage, playing music that was much slower, and the lights had been turned low, an eerie purple. The singer was a woman with a baritone voice, angelic, belting siren calls. The reverb echoed in the narrow hallway behind the stage, impossibly loud. Seph marched to the green room door and swung it open, stepping forward.

Roland followed, stumbled into a scene already in motion.

There were three teenage skinheads in leather jackets, torn white T-shirts, and they were huddled together in the far corner of the musty, wood-paneled room—all of them yelling frantically at the same time, their hands up in the air, terrified. And then there was Max, his back turned to the door, hacking at the air with a butcher knife, its blade gleaming in the light. Grigore didn't hesitate, pushed his way past Roland, stomped into the room and wrapped his arms around Max in a bear hug, pinning Max's arms against his body, demanding he drop the knife, screaming it over and over again, drop the knife, drop the fucking knife, just barely audible beneath the steady crush of the music. Two of the skinheads took the opportunity to flee, one throwing Seph out of the way and tangling with Roland, the other one scrambling down the hallway. The third one stayed frozen in the corner of the room, in shock, his hands on his head, breathing hard.

Max was rabid, tried to shake Grigore off, but Grigore had at least sixty pounds on Max, stood a head taller. The Ukrainian grabbed hold of Max's forearm, tried to shake the knife from Max's lunatic grip, slammed Max's hand against his own thigh, an awful meaty sound.

There was barely enough time to register what was happening.

Roland saw Seph down on the ground, getting up. And then the kid Roland was tangled up with clocked him in the temple, a sharp knuckle catching him just beneath the eye. The lights dimmed as he stumbled back a step, two steps forward, doomy music drowned out by a high-pitched whine. The pain was instant. By the time the room came back into focus and his head cleared, Max had dropped the knife and Grigore had thrown him onto the couch, where he lay sprawled and panting, the front of his shirt covered in blood.

Roland felt his eye beginning to swell, throbs of pain. He swooped down and picked up the knife, still trying to make sense of the scene unfolding, thinking abstractly that the knife's handle was sticky with blood. The last remaining skinhead was arguing with Seph in Ukrainian, impossible to understand what about, the two of them screaming at each other.

Max kept trying to get up from the couch and Grigore kept shoving him back down. Finally, Grigore had enough, and pulled the gun free from the waistband of his jeans, brought down the butt of the grip on Max's head, kissing a red gash just below his hairline. Then he pistol whipped Max across the side of his head, just above his ear. Dark blood gushed out from under his long hair, running down his neck.

Who the fuck did this guy think he was? The rage Roland had felt in the pit earlier that night came flooding back. This is how it was going to be. And when Grigore raised the gun, aimed the barrel between Max's eyes—getting ready to do it, finger on the trigger—Roland reached around, grabbed Grigore's arm close to the elbow, and jerked it back.

It was a miracle the gun didn't go off. Roland fully expected the gun to go off. Instead, Grigore pivoted on one foot and smashed his free hand into the side of Roland's neck, landed another blow on his ear, a third on his shoulder. Roland recognized the rage in Grigore's eyes, knew it well, remembered riding high on its blood-red wave when he'd crushed that thieving rapist's eyeball at the YMCA.

He slid the blade into Grigore's belly, just below the ribcage. The Ukrainian's eyes went wide and his mouth twisted up like he'd eaten something sour. Then Roland stuck him again. And again and again. He leaned into the last one and pulled up on the handle of the blade, twisted the knife into Grigore's guts. There was blood everywhere, flowing warm over Roland's hand. Grigore fell to one knee, dropped the gun to the floor, grabbing at Roland helplessly. His teeth were clenched, blood dribbling down his chin.

Seph had been right. When it had come time, Roland had killed without thinking.

Grigore collapsed to the floor at Roland's feet just as the band in the hall played the last note of their song, held it long and loud, letting it fade to a high-pitched whine.

Seph fell to her knees at Grigore's side.

There was a brief, thousand-ton silence, and then Roland heard the crackle of the crowd's scattered, unenthusiastic applause. He watched disinterestedly as a viscous, rust-colored bubble formed around Grigore's mouth, grew wide with his last breath, and popped cleanly, spraying a light pink mist across the floor.

8

Once the spell of roughing it in the woods wore off, Falchik, who had previously lived only in urban Kharkiv, slid steadily into boredom. He suffered restlessness during the day, complained that there was nothing to do at night. He missed the lights of the city, the radioactive blare of televisions, the drone of traffic. Such was the disease of the modern world.

Seph believed that attuning oneself to the rhythms of the moon and the sun was the only cure for this disease. She believed this because it was how she had been raised. Before her, it was how her parents had been raised. Falchik, on the other hand, proved resistant. Out here, away from the grotesque mechanisms of modern life, incurable boredom wasn't just dangerous, it was corrupting, a contagion that needed to be quarantined and eradicated. But Falchik was her friend, her band mate, and she wanted desperately to save him, not to lose him to temptation. So she attempted to explain the importance of their work again and again, until they rarely spoke of anything else. He may have been a passionate drummer, but he did not believe in the message of Wisdom's music—the thing that mattered most. He did not believe in their way of life.

Their friendship became strained. They frequently argued. Falchik didn't want to work in the fields beneath the hot sun;

he wanted to play music, smoke weed. He didn't want to help construct a new chicken coop; he wanted to drink vodka, go to shows, get laid. He believed that life was to be enjoyed, and this was his weakness.

Seph did everything she could to help him understand that there were bigger things than this world. She explained that pleasure was fleeting, honor forever. She accompanied him on long walks, visiting the holy sites, and recounted cherished folklore passed down to her by her ancestors. She made excuses for him when others on the compound complained that he avoided his fair share of work. All the while, she felt him slipping away, giving in to his disease.

It was a bright and beautiful summer morning when they discovered the rotting and swollen bodies of the two teenagers in the camper trailer, a boy and a girl, brother and sister, both of whom had stayed on as hands after the Beltane festival, runaways from somewhere in the Balkans. It didn't take long for Seph to figure it out. And Falchik, to his credit, readily admitted to his crimes. Yes, he had given them a bad batch of heroin, and yes, he had been selling drugs at the festivals, saving money in hopes of moving back to the city. No, he did not fear justice. He knew well and good that he faced the harshest of punishments, but he was not a believer. And it is impossible to fear that in which you do not believe.

Seph knew then that there was nothing she could do to save him.

Falchik's fate was a wound that had never healed. And now, as she watched Grigore's black blood pool on the floor, Seph knew that she would have to once again send a loved one before the Lord for judgment.

The walls shook as the band in the main hall tilted into their next song, the achingly low and deep rumble of funeral doom, melodramatic leads—the timing of it was so absurd it almost made her laugh, such a ridiculous soundtrack for the scene of a murder. Mark took a step toward the door, thinking he could slip out unnoticed, and suddenly Seph was on her feet, forgetting all about the music. She was livid, clawing at Mark's eyes, hammering his chest and face with her fists, thinking only of Falchik, the burden of rage she'd harbored all these years. Mark did not fight back, merely covered his face to protect himself.

It was imperative that no one outside know what had happened. If this ever got out—that a murder—no, she couldn't think of that now. Their entire way of life was at stake. She needed to remain calm, be strong.

Roman swept into the room, nearly shoving Seph out of the way, followed by a few others. Somebody slammed shut the door. Everyone was yelling, shoving. She thought she heard Max laughing. Could that possibly be true? Was he really that cruel? She saw Roman wrestle the knife away from Roland. Then she felt a hand grab her by the arm—the smell of sulfur filling her nostrils—wiry strength pulling her away. She rushed down the narrow hallway and out the back door, cool air washing away the heat of panic and blood. Her legs were weak, shook slightly as she stood beneath the spinning and starry sprawl of the nighttime sky. Taras shut the door and turned to her, that all-knowing look on his long, gray face.

His tired eyes said it all—everything she needed to know. And so she followed him deep into the heart of the compound. She knew exactly where he was taking her: the same place they'd taken Falchik.

All the while, the band kept playing, the music never stopped.

The festival continued.

Taras and Seph entered the shipping container through its wide double doors. A single light bulb within an industrial cage hung from the ceiling, casting striped shadows along the corrugated steel walls. Taras leaned down and threw back the hatch installed in the cement floor, unearthing the smell of dust, recycled air. Seph was first to descend the metal ladder, the sounds of her boots on the ladder's rungs echoing, and disappear into the blackened depths of the bunker. Taras followed after her, pulling the hatch shut behind him.

The low lights flickered on, revealing a tight maze of cold, concrete hallways. Seph hid herself away in a small, dark room. She lay facedown on the cot and wept, the damp spots on the stiff sheets growing as large as fists, larger still. Exhausted, she fell into feverish sleep. She dreamt of being buried alive, down in the center of the earth where there was nothing but darkness, empty caves collapsing all around her, helplessly crushed by the weight of the world above.

Moments later, perhaps hours—time seemed to move at its own, peculiar pace in the bunker—Taras's solemn voice reached out to her from the darkness. "He's ready for you now."

She entered the room, alone, and shut the door. Cold fluorescents hummed. Roland sat on a steel-frame bed, which was bolted to the wall, its only comfort a thin rubber mattress. Black jailhouse bars divided the room in two. Seph sat in the wooden chair opposite Roland in his cell. He looked terrible, pale and shaken. The skin around his watery eyes was puffy, inflamed, and his hands were still stained red with Grigore's blood.

The white noise of the bunker filters whirred softly.

No part of her wanted to have this talk.

"Do you know why you're here?" she asked.

He quickly stood, stepped forward and held the bars. "It was an accident, Seph," he said, his voice hoarse, desperate. The muscles in his arms tensed, but the cell had been built firm, the bars embedded deep within the concrete. "Please, you have to

believe me. He was out of control. He was going to kill Max."
She let him continue. He seemed to be struggling for the right
words. "He was going to kill my friend. I couldn't let that happen."

So they were friends now.

It took all of her strength to remain impassive, cool. "Sit
down."

"Seph, please, let me out of here." Again, his muscles tensed.
"It was an accident."

She repeated herself, slowly this time. "Sit... down."

His eyes narrowed. He was starting to understand that she
was not here to comfort him, that she was not his visitor, but
his captor. His head dropped and his hands fell away from the
bars. He stumbled back to the bed, took a seat. He no longer looked her in the eye, sullen, leaning forward, head in his
hands.

She waited a moment. "Let's begin again. Do you know why
you're here?"

"You can't hold me here," he said, suddenly angry. He looked
up at her and his gaze was electric, tears rolling over his flushed
cheeks. His voice quavered as he spoke. "I'm an American. I
have rights. You have to call the police and explain what happened."

"We will not be calling the police."

"This isn't right. You can't keep me here."

"We do not intend to. Once the festival ends, you'll be taken
away from here."

"To the police?"

Seph sighed. "The police cannot help you, Roland. You have
committed a serious crime, a crime beyond the jurisdiction of
men. You have spilled blood on holy land. You have broken a
sacred law. And for that you must face judgment."

"I don't understand."

"I will do my best to explain, because I believe you are owed that much. I ask only that you listen closely and take my words seriously. Can you promise me that?"

"Seph, I—"

"Please, just promise."

He nodded. "OK. I promise."

She told Roland a folktale from her childhood, a story passed down from generation to generation, one which she herself had been told countless times. She hoped that it would help him understand his situation, the seriousness of his transgression.

It begins in the medieval ages, a time of darkness and despair. Princes and dukes rule the lands, waging war with one another, though it is the subjects of the kingdoms who suffer the most. Young men are plucked from the safety of their villages and forced to carry banners for bloodthirsty warlords who do not know their names. Women are regarded as nothing more than the spoils of war. They are raped, slaughtered, sold as slaves. The children of fallen foes are massacred, burned and buried in unmarked graves.

The fields run red with the blood of the peasants. Workers are unable to tend to the crops and famine quickly spreads—ushering in the great black cloud of death. The princes and dukes kill one another unmercifully until only the strongest remain, spread far throughout the lands. The fighting between the kingdoms ends, and in its place emerges sovereign rule, a new life of servitude and protection. Maps are drawn and borders are established. Each new kingdom is assigned to a ruler, a voivode of limitless power.

Here, in these woods, reigns Lord Drevylan, a legendary warrior and supposed practitioner of the dark arts. With no one to challenge his rule, the Lord seals himself away in the keep of the high castle beneath the moon, where he seeks to join the gods of old as a constellation in the nighttime sky. He summons to his side a mysterious man known only as the black magician, a man from the far reaches of the earth and beyond. The black magician is a heretic, a descendant of others much like him. He aids the Lord with his spells and each day the Lord grows stronger. Yet the more power the Lord accrues, the less human he becomes. Soon even his own men do not recognize the sound of his voice.

But they do his bidding all the same. Under the banner of the golden trident, a group of Drevylan's warriors convene in the high castle beneath the moon, in celebration of darkest night, the winter solstice. Granted speed and strength by the black magician, they ride their red-eyed horses through the forest, from village to village, town to town, seeking remuneration for their Lord's protection: the villagers' firstborn sons and daughters.

It goes on like this for centuries.

Then, on a night when the moon is full and the snow deep, Drevylan unlocks the great secret of the gods of old, the secret of the stars. He clears the path to ascend and wages war on the primordial being—chaos itself, the bornless one—unleashing the black miasma that covers the world. The war is long and it is difficult but ultimately the Lord is crowned the victor. And as such he becomes all-knowing, ever-seeing, the protector of our lands.

From that day forward, He reigns supreme as the Lord of lords, ruler of the Black Sea, and bringer of peace. And we are all his children. His blood is our blood, the blood of the land's firstborn son and daughters. He provides the air we breathe, the water we drink, the food we eat, and in doing so, he lives forever within each of us. And in death we return our bodies to the earth, joining our flesh to his flesh, the Lord Leviathan.

She finished speaking and sat back in the chair. Her heart fluttered in her chest. Each time she told this tale, it roused her spirits, made her swell with pride and a sense of belonging.

Roland spoke almost immediately. "Your lord is a sea monster?"

"Christian lies," she said, taken aback by the question, the tone of his voice. It was so snide, so arrogant—so utterly American. Had he not understood the beauty of the tale? Could he not see its implications? "The Christians created the image of the sea monster in an attempt to give form to the formless, hid their beast beneath dark waves where no man could find it and prove it false. That is what they do, they lie. They obscure reality. They are antilife. The truth is that they could not fathom the limitlessness of the beyond. It did not adhere to their pathetic conception of the afterlife." She paused. "They did get one thing right, however. It is the mouth of Leviathan that will swallow the world during the last judgment. But not for any of the reasons they believe." Another pause. "Let me ask you, do you know why it is named the Black Sea?"

Roland shook his head.

"It is named for the nighttime sky, the black and unknowable abyss that surrounds our world. It is one of thousands of other seas, millions actually, all connected in the cosmic web. He slips into and through all worlds, always at war with others like him. Such is the realm of Leviathan, the infinite worlds beyond our own, the unknowable depths between worlds, the darkness between the stars."

Roland sat in stunned silence. "You're a crazy person," he said.

They stared at one another.

Just days before, when they looked into one another's eyes, Seph had felt a wondrous connection, had heard unspoken words of affection and longing. And yet today, she saw only a scared and closed-minded little man. Maybe she had mis-judged him. Maybe he was not open to her way of living after all, her beliefs. How could she have been so wrong?

Silence fell between them like a curtain, and in that silence she heard only the white noise of the bunker filters, the hum of the fluorescents, everywhere and nowhere. Roland had shrunken into himself, his shoulders pulled forward, back rounded. He looked so small. He looked weak. It made her want to crush him.

And then he laughed, his voice booming in the small room. It was the laughter of someone losing their grip on reality, both frightened and hysterical. "You really believe all this shit? You're fucking nuts." Suddenly he was on his feet again and his voice was filled with rage. "Get me the fucking police, you fucking psycho bitch."

"I'm sorry," she said softly, ignoring him, his anger. And truly, she was sorry. She felt for him just as she had felt for Falchik. But those feelings of sympathy had done little to bring Falchik back from wherever it was he had gone, just as her feelings now for Roland were of no use. She stood, turned her back to him, no longer hearing his pleas for mercy, for forgiveness, his calling her name again and again, and left him there, alone.

Never again did she expect to see Roland alive and as she had known him, if she had ever really known him at all.

9

They entered Roland's cell, Roman and the others, surrounded him, and forced him down on the bed. Someone palmed the side of his skull, held him down. They bent his arms back, taped his wrists together, taped his ankles together, pulled a black wool cap over his head, plunging him into a world of darkness. Then they dragged him outside and threw him in the back of an empty van, stripped down to its cold metal floor, slid shut the door.

He couldn't see shit, could barely breathe through the thick wool. His hands tingled, swollen with blood. Maybe three or four other people climbed into the van. Everyone spoke Ukrainian, voices low and direct, nothing Roland could make out. The doors slammed shut. The engine turned over. Spooky dungeon synth pumped through the speakers. Somebody cracked open a beer, then another, another—like it was just a joyride with the guys. The van's tires skidded out on the ice. Roland worried he was going to break his neck on a sharp turn, and then a sharp turn sent him careening into what must have been the driver's seat, nearly tore his shoulder from its socket. Everyone laughed. Somebody grabbed hold of his legs and pulled him back into the center of the van. Then somebody else held him in place. Then somebody else slowly poured out a beer on his head, saturating the wool cap, turning it into a death mask.

Roland struggled to breathe. Blood pulsed through his neck. Heavy black stones pushed at the backs of his eyeballs. And then it was over and he could breathe again, could just barely pull a breath through the wet fabric, just barely enough oxygen to lift the heavy stones. When the overwhelming thump of his heartbeat faded, he heard that everyone was laughing again.

It was like he was trapped in a horror movie, a stupid torture-porn flick. How many movies had he seen like this? And never once had he thought about what it might feel like—to be the victim, to be toyed with—because those movies never seemed real. They were too stupid to be real, just exaggerations of violence. Just like none of this could possibly be real. It was too exaggerated, too stupid. Everything Seph had said earlier, all that crazy cult talk, she was just fucking with him, right? This was some kind of prank, maybe even an initiation. They'd drive him out to the woods, march him through the snow, get him nice and scared, make him think he was about to die, then they'd pull off the stupid fucking wool cap, and—

And what? Hand him a shot of vodka, clap him on the back, and welcome him to the tribe? No fucking way. Not after what he'd done. Not after he'd killed one of their own.

He started to cry, just started sobbing his fucking eyes out. He couldn't help himself. Everyone stopped laughing. Someone yelled over the music and the music got even louder. After that they left him alone. They stopped messing with him, just held him in place on the turns, made sure he didn't get hurt. Every so often he heard the sound of another beer being cracked open. Every bump in the road pummeled his bones through the van's naked metal floor. One song bled into the next, a stream of haunting melodies, until finally the van slowed, stopped, and the music cut, a sudden vacuum filled only by a mournful ringing in his ears.

The door slid open and there were hands all over him, under his arms, the bend of his knees, his waist. They hoisted him out of the van and then unceremoniously dropped him into the snow. The beer-soaked wool hat instantly shrunk in the cold air, clung to every contour of his face. It was harder to breathe than ever and Roland shook his head back and forth in vain, grunting, doing whatever he could to loosen the death mask's skin-tight fit.

"Don't move," someone said, followed by the unmistakably metal-sharp sound of a long knife being drawn from its canvas sheath.

Roland wiggled in the snow bed, tried to get up, get free, but managed only to lodge himself deeper. "No," he said, "please."

God, what did he think they were going to do? Gut him right there in the snow?

He heard a sawing sound, the sound of a blade biting into rope, five quick back-and-forth slashes, twitch-quick, barely had time to register that his ankles were no longer bound to-gether, when off came the death mask. The world around him opened. He was deep in the dark woods. It was like shooting awake in the morning after a blackout, panic-stricken, every-thing twisted and unfamiliar. He filled his lungs with cold air and erupted into a cascading coughing fit.

When the coughing fit passed, he opened his half-frozen eyes, and was blinded by the cool blare of a flashlight.

"Please," he said again, trying to make out the faces occulted by the light. He could just barely see the dark and shifting shapes of several other people, the saw-blade silhouettes of pine trees cutting into the night.

"From here you walk," Roman said. He slid a machete back into its scabbard, its polished blade briefly glinting in the light of the moon. And then, addressing the group, said something in Ukrainian, gave some kind of order, because two of the others stepped forward and grabbed Roland beneath each arm, pulled him into a standing position.

His legs wobbled beneath his weight, unresponsive, unsure.

"If you try to run," Roman said, "we cut off a finger. And still you will have to walk."

Roland's legs moved of their own volition, his body wholly separate from his mind, which was paralyzed by stinging, slow-dripping fear. He leaned forward slightly into each step, wiggled his fingers every so often, trying to keep the blood flowing.

He recognized his surroundings as soon as his eyes adjusted to the eerie blue glow of the darkened forest, just as he remembered it, rolling with sluggish moon fog. He remembered the high outcroppings of stone, the limitless black-portal sky. More than anything he remembered the unearthly silence, the way sounds seemed isolated from one another, depressed. They had taken him back to the Valley of Many Sorrows. He was back at the beginning again, a pointless circle. It was just a bad dream. A nightmare. One of the men walking behind him did an uncanny impression of a wolf howling at the moon. And then all the others started howling. Roland slowed and someone shoved him forward. He fell to his knees, got up quickly, and kept marching forward.

In a weird way, the landscape calmed him. It was impossible to ignore its beauty, its pristine snows and brilliantly cold colors. He swelled with a sudden understanding that the world he had always known was nothing more than an illusion, a façade of shifting lights, motion, and sounds. He'd never had any control of his life—and this was where his anger had come from, that he was nothing, a tertiary character stuck in a cluttered background.

God, why was he only realizing this now?

The valley deepened, the night darkened.

Soon enough they came to one of the impossibly tall breaking wheels and Roland was again reminded of Bruegel's *The Triumph of Death*. It fell upon him that he'd always understood the painting superficially. From the poor to the rich, death spared no one.

He had spent his life as the fool, inattentive, banging his drums, unmindful of the horrors that loomed mockingly over his shoulder, always destined to come to no good.

Grigore had said that a man who lost touch with his soul suffered a fate worse than death. At the time, Roland hadn't understood what that meant. Now he was starting to get an idea. And for the first time since he'd made the decision to end Grigore's life, Roland thought of Max. What had happened to him? Where had they taken him?

A massive and scorched rock wall rose before them, emerging from the snow-swept darkness all at once. They had reached the end of their long journey. Roland looked up at what appeared to be the curtain wall of a castle, maybe twenty or thirty feet high, tightly stacked with blackened bricks. It was difficult to separate the wall from the night itself, one bleeding into the other, yet there it was all the same. Low winds whistled through the valley, lightly dusting the black stones with powdery snow. Roman angled his flashlight toward a snaking chasm in the wall, which widened where it met the ground.

One of the others stepped forward and, with a quick flick of a small blade, cut through the tape holding Roland's wrists together. Roland rubbed feeling back into his wrists. His shoulders were packed with tightness, aching dully.

"You will continue through here," Roman said, gesturing toward the crack in the wall. "We cannot go past this point.

From here you are on your own."

It dawned on Roland what this meant. "You can't be serious," he said. "What is this?"

"The dungeons of the high castle," Roman said.

Someone behind Roland pushed him lightly in the direction of the wall.

"Go," Roman said. "And may the Lord watch over you."

What other choice did he have? With his head down, he walked through the snow and approached the blackened wall, lowering his shoulder and turning sideways to fit within the crooked crevice. It was a tight squeeze, the cold stone digging into his arched back, scraping his bent knees. He shuffled sideways for four, maybe five feet. The stone released its grip and he realized that he could stand upright within the darkness.

Inside was a vacuum of silence—the wind silenced. He took a few tentative steps, half expecting to plummet into a pit, to be impaled on a bed of stakes, to splash into a vat of acid. But the ground remained firm beneath his feet.

At first he worried that he shared this dark space with another, a shrunken madman grinding his horrible teeth. And when he realized that it was not the sound of teeth grinding, but rather the sound of stone grinding against stone, when he realized that Roman and the others were sliding into place a large stone plate over the crevice in the wall, he couldn't help but wonder if his mind had made one last attempt at protecting his sanity. He flung his body at the stone, scratching at it with his nails, banging on it with his fists, screaming. He searched out the crevice in the darkness, tried to crawl back through, to escape before they locked him away for good, only now he wouldn't fit, he was somehow too big.

The panic set in after that, utterly paralyzing. He had never known total and complete darkness until this moment, had never known pure terror, sealed within the black stones of the high castle's dungeon in a faraway country, on this, winter's longest night.

PART THREE
FIELDS OF
PUNISHMENT

1

Likho ducked his head through the milking stool's legs and raised it from the ground. Hobbling a few uneven steps at a time, he transported the stool from one end of the barn to the other. He placed it near the door, climbed onto it—his upright tail flicking back and forth—and with a single clumsy hoof released the latch. Then he freed the door from its frame with his nose, stepped down onto his two front legs, and pushed out into the world beyond.

His hunger was impossible to ignore, as it always was, grinding away dully, compelling him forward. The enticing smells of pungent garbage and charcoal lingered in the crisp morning air. He cautiously raised a floppy ear before deciding that it was safe to proceed, bounding into the immense open space, free to do as he pleased, take as he wished. The sun had not yet risen and pale smoke rose like ghosts from the scattered fires, abandoned to smolder overnight after the festival. He approached the charred ring of the nearest fire pit, bowed his head to the ground, and rotated his single eye. The world he knew was warped, colorless. Everything he did he did by ancient instinct, unthinking, wanting only to consume and to do so unbothered, far away from the oily stink of his ugly masters. He chewed loudly on a small piece of charcoal, breaking it down into a soft, chalky paste, swallowing. The smoky scorched flavor was strong and bitter, connecting him to the remnants of the flame, the father, that terrible thing that blackens wood and cleanses the world. His mind flooded with visions of scorched forests, swirling pits of molten stone, bloodshed and wrath. He bleated with joy. When he was done, he rolled in the comfort of the soft ashes, coating his black fur in the dust of unbecoming.

Likho aimlessly followed the smells that drifted in the light winds, quickly losing interest in those that were familiar, un-exciting, and pursuing only the strange, the ever more alluring. He went farther out than he'd ever been before, bounding into the deep snow.

Here he picked up a new smell, something powerful. The memories it loosened ran deep. He was gifted flashes of the world as a bloated corpse, filled to bursting with putrefying gases. He saw the ragged forms of small furry animals weather-ing in time-lapse until there was only tooth and bone. He saw the discolored and rotting husk of a dead whale rising to the surface of the sea, nipped at by countless gulls, sharks tearing away great chunks of meat.

Likho did not understand what these words meant, or how to translate these images into knowledge. He understood nothing beyond animal instinct, the impulse to burrow deep under the skin of the dead and dying, to gnaw free the fleshy nutrients offered to him, to rip away life, grow stronger, take and kill and take some more. It was this impulse that brought him to the building removed from all of the others, the lone building out in the deep snow.

The door was shut. He bayed in frustration. It was yet another obstacle, something he'd have to figure out. Nothing could ever be his without effort. He sniffed at the door inquisitively, overwhelmed by the nearness of whatever it was that emitted such an intoxicating odor—such a lovely smell of rot. He bleated. Still the door stood fast. He scratched at it, pushed his snout into it, bleated again and again. And when it finally swung open, Likho looked up with his single eye, elated, only to see the ugly master, the one who wore black, who stank of the oils of the forest.

He was terrified of the one who wore black, for in those dark swirling clouds the man breathed, Likho was given to see scenes of animal sacrifice, so many others like him gutted and swinging bleeding from hooks high in the trees.

The little black goat turned and fled.

2

Max tried to sit up in the darkness, only to remember that he had been restrained, bound with leather, his wrists and ankles strapped to the bed posts.

He thrashed his legs to the point of exhaustion. His muscles were packed with lactic acid. He couldn't remember the last time he'd brushed his teeth. He tried to laugh again but heard that he was crying, and when he opened up and let himself weep, he found that he was laughing.

In the next room he heard the sound of a door slam shut, Taras's muffled voice yelling something.

His pulse quickened. Where the fuck was he? An ornate light fixture in the ceiling lit up, tasting of scorched dust. Pain ricocheted in his skull. His eyes stung. He saw that he was in a small, well-furnished room, still wearing his boots. He'd pissed the bed.

The door to his room opened, the floorboards creaked. Suddenly Taras loomed over him like a dark tower, dressed all in flowing black, reeking of tobacco leaves and spoiled meat. His thin gray beard was discolored from smoking.

"So you're awake," he said, chuckling. "You slept the sleep of the dead."

"Where's Roland?" Max said, barely able to crack open his sore jaw. The hoarseness of his voice alarmed him. How long had he been in this room, slipping in and out of consciousness?

But Taras paid him no mind. He'd turned his back, hunched forward slightly. He fiddled with something in his hands. When he turned around again, Max saw he held a syringe, its barrel a lovely and warm yellowish brown. A jet of liquid arced from the needle.

Max's mouth flooded with saliva and his temples throbbed with the slow grind of his exhausted heart. The heat of expectation rose in his throat.

"What is that?"

"This?" Taras said innocently, looking at the syringe as if he were surprised to see it there. "This is what you wanted, of course. What you called out for in your sleep. Now please relax. I've come to take your pain away."

Taras unlaced one of Max's boots, pulled it off, removed the sock. The needle slid in between two toes. A moment later and it was done. The spiders were all gone. His heart sang, gushed. He'd never known such mercy.

"Now, if I undo your restraints," Taras said, "will you promise to behave yourself?"

Max nodded dreamily.

After he'd been freed, Max ran his hands over his head, which had been shaved. He picked disinterestedly at a scab on his forehead, ran his finger along the stitched cut above his ear. Taras explained that they'd had to cut off all of his hair to give him stitches, that his wounds were deep, requiring medical attention. Max went to the wall and looked into a picture frame, using the glass as a mirror. Both of his eyes were blacked. He looked like Uncle Fester.

"You will follow me, please," Taras said. "Your presence has been requested."

They shuffled slowly down a narrow hallway, Taras smelling ever more strongly of smoke and incense. Gilt-framed oil paintings—their subject matter dark and smudged, vaguely menacing—crowded the paneled walls. The warped floorboards creaked in the musty silence. Despite the brightly burning, ornate silver candelabra, the high ceiling was obscured by shadow. At the end of the hallway, Taras turned, unlocked a door with a long, thin key, one of dozens he kept on a ring, and stepped forward into the shadows. And there, in the space that had so suddenly opened up, hanging high and proud above a candle-covered wooden shrine, Max laid eyes on the portrait of the man whose face he had seen blotting out the sky, the man whose skin crawled with wretched life.

Bits and pieces came back. He remembered slipping on the ice, junk-sick and stir-crazy, hitting his head. He remembered slapping that poor little girl across the face, the weight of the butcher knife in his hand, and the look of utter ferocity on Grigore's face as he raised his pistol into the air, ready to rain down a hammer blow. And the rest... Well, that would likely return on its own. His memory always did have a way of asserting itself when it was least useful.

Max took a few steps closer to better read the engraved gold plaque mounted on the painting's frame. "Drevylan—Lord Leviathan." He studied the portrait. The man had small features set in a wide, reddish face. His dark hair formed a widow's peak. He did not smile and his eyes were an all-consuming black, like a shark's. In the foreground, a spool of golden thread unraveled near the subject's hand, and a red candle burned brightly, its flame haloed with light. The background was composed of roiling colors, an apocalyptic atmosphere, orange bleeding into red, which cooled into purplish blue.

"I see you are admiring our portrait of Lord Drevylan," Taras said from the other room. He took a step forward out of the shadows, standing in the doorway, smiling crookedly. "You have remarkable taste. That portrait is priceless, the only one of its kind."

"I've seen this man before," Max said.

The smirk on Taras's face fell away. "I'm afraid that is not possible," he said. "As I said, this portrait is unique—the only known likeness of Drevylan in existence. Surely, you've not been here before?"

"No, not this painting," Max said, "but his actual face. I saw it filling the sky, stretched out everywhere." He thought hard about how to describe what he had seen. He had been between two places, in a dark void. The words did not come easily. How could he describe something so extraordinary? "His skin was moving, writhing, like it was stitched together with thousands of broken people."

Taras stared sternly at Max, as if thinking this over. When he did speak, his voice was soft, filled with emotion. "It is no coincidence, your being here. I have known this to be true for quite some time. He has called to you, shown Himself to you. He brought you to us because He believes you have a purpose. This is what the stones predicted and the stones do not lie." He paused. "Please, let's continue. Seph is waiting."

She sat in an old plush chair in what appeared to be some kind of drawing room, her legs crossed, her hair pulled back in a severe ponytail. The ceiling was molded, the walls paneled. An intricate red-and-black carpet spanned the floor. And on the wall behind her was mounted a massive pair of crossed two-handed swords behind the crest of the golden trident.

Taras went to her, knelt at her side, and whispered in her ear. When he was finished, she seemed to regard Max differently, her face slack with dumb fascination.

"Please sit," Seph said, gesturing to the leather sofa.

"What is this place?" he said, scanning the room. Vitrines had been assembled along one wall, containing any manner of artifacts, and a brass telescope as large as a bazooka sat before one of the iron-gated windows, angled toward the sky. In the far corner of the room sat a wooden navigator's globe, the shapes of its map on first glance looking entirely unfamiliar.

"Every culture does what it can to preserve its way of life," Seph said. "This house was once inhabited by an heir to the Lord's estate. It has since been turned into something of a museum, a reminder of our shared history. I wanted you to see this—to meet me here—so you would better understand what is at stake."

He stood before one of the vitrines. A thin curved blade was laid out upon a tasseled felt pillow, its handle intricately carved ivory, or perhaps even bone, stained with blotchy discolorations. On the wall, he saw a framed photograph, badly blurred. He could just barely make out the shapes of several black-cloaked figures, the shapes of crooked trees. One of the wraiths held against his chest—its blade gleaming in the light—the very same curved blade.

"An old ceremonial object," Seph said. "Very rare."

Max turned. She gestured to him to sit.

He sank deep into the couch and was suddenly thirsty, suddenly aware of how truly foul he smelled. He heard Taras quietly shut the door, disappearing discreetly.

Seph turned slightly in her seat, extending an arm to her side, gesturing to the room. "Everything you see here has meaning. And it is my responsibility to preserve that meaning, to ensure that our history is not forgotten." Her voice tightened and her eyes narrowed. "Do you understand what I have sacrificed? Toiling day after day in the fields, growing food, making sure no one goes hungry. Getting out of bed when it's still dark outside and milking the cows. These tasks have taken a toll on my body—my back, my hands—but still I work because I have wanted nothing more than to strengthen this community, to provide. Then you come along, and in less than two weeks you threaten to undo all of that hard work."

He was in no mood for a lecture.

"Where's Roland?" Max said.

Seph cleared her throat, startled. "He is gone."

"Where?"

"That does not concern you," Seph said. She leaned forward, spoke forcefully. "Let me explain something to you. Here we abide by laws. Do you understand the difference between rules and laws? No? The difference is that rules suppress, laws liberate. Rules are easily broken, whereas laws are sacred. You haven't just broken the rules, Max. You can't simply be slapped on the wrist. You have violated any number of our laws. As a result of this, you are no longer our guest. You have forfeited your rights to ask questions and to receive answers. From now on you do as you're told—nothing more. In exchange for your cooperation, we will keep you supplied with what you need. Do you understand?"

Who the fuck did she think she was, talking to him like that? No fucking woman was going to tell him how it was, not without a fight.

He wanted to get up off this couch and punch her in the fucking mouth. But the drugs flowing through his blood wouldn't let him. His eyelids felt heavy. He felt sick, awash in the throes of a world-class hangover. He tried to remember what happened, what had brought him here, but recalled only blackness, a vague sense of despair, as if whole episodes of his memory had been wiped clean, erased.

Every time he shut his eyes he saw that horrible face stretched across the sky, those yellowed eyes radiating something like quaking madness.

"Your sole focus from now on will be your music," Seph said. "Taras has been communicating with your record label on your behalf. He has told them that you are writing songs, that your material is coming together nicely. You will work uninterrupted and remain on the compound. Twice a day Taras will visit you and administer your medication. You will take your meals with him so he can ensure that you are eating."

"I don't have anything written," Max said. "The kid was—"

"That is not my concern. You are not new to this, Strigoi. I am sure you can put something together that will be to your exacting standards. You will need to start recording demos soon. This will happen here, in the rehearsal hall." She leaned back in the chair. Her voice softened. "Everything has been arranged. You merely need to do what you do best. There is a special plan for you in this world, Strigoi. It is time for you to accept that as your reality."

And with that, Max was dismissed.

Taras materialized behind him, placing a bony hand on his shoulder. The two of them went down another dark, crowded hallway until they came to a windowless, stainless-steel door.

"There is one more thing for you to see," Taras said.

They entered a cold, white-tiled room with a cement floor. The room smelled strongly of disinfectant, but beneath that smell, barely concealed, the sickeningly sweet rot of apples—the stench of death—stomach-churning putrescence. Sterile white lights buzzed in the ceiling. Three men wearing surgical masks, black aprons, and brown-smeared latex gloves stood around a stainless-steel table, all of them looking up in unison, surprised by the sudden intrusion. One of them raised a single hand, palm forward, as if to deter Taras and Max from coming any closer.

If the masked men were trying to hide what was on the table, then it was already too late. At first, Max didn't know what he was looking at. It looked like a bad prop from an old Hammer Frankenstein movie, a waxy mannequin, a misshapen mound of wet clay. But this was no mannequin; it was too detailed, too realistic. There, on top of the table, feet pointing toward the ceiling, lay Grigore's naked, gray-skinned corpse. A Y-shaped incision had been drawn from the top of each shoulder, pulled down to the navel. His insides had been scraped clean, and the purple and red tissues of the torso's cavity gleamed smoothly like the inside of a mouth. A metal bin on a rolling table nearly overflowed with lumps of unidentifiable viscera.

Max turned and barely made it to the deep sink along the wall, brought up an incredibly painful thin stream of bile. His headache was back in full force.

And with it everything else came back in a rush, the black vacuum in his mind flooded with color and sound, everything he'd wanted to forget. He remembered finding Mark and his shithead bandmates in the shitty little green room, the slow-pounding doom band rumbling as huge as thunderheads. Again he saw that look of ferocity on Grigore's face, saw him raise up that pistol, racking the slide and chambering the bullet, only this time he remembered that in the next moment, Roland pulled back Grigore's arm. And then he remembered Grigore's body slumping to the floor, falling sideways, hemorrhaging blood black as scorched oil.

Taras's voice reached him as if through a dark and twisting tunnel. "Not feeling so good, Strigoi?" he said. "Surely the man who bears such a name, *Strigoi*, who has fashioned himself after those who have risen from the grave, the tortured and the cursed, is not troubled by simple death. Surely such a man would understand this."

Max wiped his mouth with his sleeve. He looked back at Taras over his shoulder. The man in black stood with his arms crossed, turned slightly, chin tilted upward, somehow appearing larger than before, as if he hovered a few inches in the air.

"There is nothing to fear," Taras said, sweeping his arm to the side, his tattered black robe hanging loose like a scabbed wing. "This man's spirit awaits new life in the black beyond. And you, fortunately, shall bear witness to his transformation."

3

Two days—Roland plucked this fact from somewhere deep in the recesses of his panicked mind—two days was how long it took for a person lost in total darkness, engulfed in complete silence, to feel their mind warped forever by nothing more than the sounds of their body, the passage of air, the pumping of fluids.

It was more than enough time to figure out what he needed to do, to figure out how to break out of here, get help, get far, far away. After all, Roland had always prided himself on his presence of mind, what others called his hard-headedness, his unwillingness to give in to the absurdities of everyday life, all the little mundane things that build up and trap you in—blocks of black stone—until you're just another fucking criminal, desperate to get free. And then what? Out there in the world, that wasn't freedom. How could it be? Out there, that's where it was really dangerous. And to think that some people actually think that keeping a person locked up for twenty-three hours is cruel and unusual. The weak-minded, you throw them in a cage for more than a day or two and they'll start seeing bugs climbing the walls, they'll open up their veins and write cryptic messages on the walls with their blood. They're weak. One hour of sunlight seemed like more than enough to keep the mind sharp, to keep the walls from fading to black. He'd kill for one hour of sunlight. He wasn't like them, the worthless sacks of shit who got gobbled up by the system, whose minds rusted over like defunct machines. Nope, he wasn't like them at all. He wasn't a killer. Roland was a fucking king—the ruler of the underworld. His living skeleton would stride through the night as if it were a twitching and blood-soaked battlefield because the dead can never die. He just had to keep this thought somewhere safe, think it over and over again, the dead can never die. He had to keep his mind sharp. There was no need for walls. It was the mind that told the body what to do. Without the mind, the body wouldn't even know to keep breathing, keep pumping blood, to keep doing those simple stupid things—those things that would supposedly drive a person to the brink of insanity with their very sound.

When he was younger he played a game where he'd walk through a familiar space, like the hallway at school, see how far he could get with his eyes closed before he ran into something. But he never did run into anything, did he? He always opened his eyes before that. Chickenshit. He was too scared of hurting himself.

How odd, then, to think that the mind would give out long before the body starved and shut down, unable to carry out such simple, automatic functions, the very things it had evolved to do unthinkingly. He had always thought of the body as the mind's prison. Now, unable to see his own hand before his face, he wasn't quite so sure.

He screamed as long and loud as was physically possible.

Would an object discarded into the vacuum of outer space continue accelerating forever? He didn't know the answer. A severed head skirting along the heavy lip of the universe. He balled up his fists and punched himself in the face over and over again, pulled his hair, screamed into the darkness. It was just a game, really. No one ever got hurt for real. The dead can never die. He opened his eyes and put out his shaking hands, placed his palms against cool stone, smooth to the touch, somehow knowing that he now stood before a wall. Chickenshit. He felt his brain smoothing over, face throbbing. And then the world seemed to shift beneath him, turned over. He wasn't standing at all. He was on his hands and knees, collapsed, crawling in the dark. He rolled onto his side, still struggling to breathe, and watched as an entire galaxy of stars opened up above him, great spiraling clouds of purple and blue gases churning slowly at an angle around a deep black disc. And there, along its lip, a tiny human head rolling end over end, laughing soundlessly, a voyager in the night.

Was it his? He couldn't bear it. He wouldn't be able to bear it if it was his.

The whole vision disappeared—just like that—an apparition swallowed up by the hungry darkness. He was starting to lose his shit, wasn't he? His fucking face hurt. He listened to the sound of his breathing, felt his pulse racing. Fuck. Maybe he wasn't as strong as he thought he was. Fucking pussy. He heard Max's voice rattle through his mind, thick with splutter and decay, repeating over and over again that Roland was a pussy, that he didn't know anything about death, what it felt like to be dead. Only it wasn't Max's voice, was it, it was Seph's voice, wasn't it, his onetime lover, void of emotion, once more reciting her psychotic little folktale. And this wasn't just a figment of his imagination—no, he could actually hear her.

"Seph?" he called, his voice ringing out in the emptiness. "Seph, are you here?"

He crawled along the frigid stone on his hands and knees, laughing at himself, the absurdity of all this, following the sound of her voice, listening closely.

A new world revealed itself, all the colors of the dark as vivid as in dreams, stripping away the shadows. He saw lines take form, sculpting with light, building shapes, swirls of color that settled into something familiar. There was the sky, looking sour. And there, in the distance, a black-branched tree as wide as a house, stuffed with stony, fat-bodied crows. The ground beneath his hands, he saw, was now soil and stones, clumps of grass, warm to the touch. And before him, a road that snaked through wild brush, carved by what had to have been wagon wheels, grassy median in its center. Seph's voice continued its murmuring, breathing life into this world, conjuring images that took shape before Roland's eyes. There was the sun, eclipsed by the moon, radiating a ring of light that somehow caused no discomfort.

Was any of this real? He rubbed a pinch of soil between two fingers, felt its fine grains roll along the surface of his skin, and watched them scatter in the wind.

It had to be real.

Roland stood, felt the breeze on his skin. He listened to the mindless calls of birds, closed his eyes, expecting everything to disappear. When he opened them again, he instead saw a co-balt-blue stream cutting its way through the ground nearby, its stony babble plinking. He smelled the freshness of the water. A wooden footbridge fell into place plank by plank. Next a small medieval-looking village spiraled into existence, its many huts built of gray stone with peaked, straw-lined roofs. In the grassy center of the village, there rose a single-room church, freshly whitewashed, with a high steeple and bell tower. And there in the distance, over the small hill, a hand-laid stone wall.

Snow fell through the air, only it couldn't be snow. It was far too warm. Roland held out his hand, watched as the fat flakes clung to his skin and smeared like grease. No, it wasn't snow at all—it was ash. He looked to an empty and abandoned horse-drawn cart alongside a pile of chopped wood and saw that its bed was suddenly stuffed with stiff corpses stacked high.

Just beyond the cart he saw the earth give way, a massive pit opening its wide mouth, walls sloping steeply into a twisted pile of even more blue-skinned corpses—men, women, children, a snarling horse frozen in rictus—and he saw, to his horror, that they were on fire, and that this fire now let off heaps of poisonous purple smoke that rained down ash from the sky.

Was he doing this? Was he just filling in the details with his imagination?

Searing heat hit him like a wall. Great clouds of smoke filled the sky, hanging low like a fog, and within their churning, noxious folds, Roland saw that the hungry yellow flames had engulfed the church, its skeletal frame blackened, licked by the fire, and that these flames had now leapt to a few of the surrounding huts, their straw roofs going up like tinderboxes. And although the roar of the church fire was all-consuming, he was still able to hear the voices of men and women calling out for help, screaming in terror.

"They're coming," someone said. "They descend from the hills."

Roland fell to the ground, smoke stinging his eyes, filling his lungs. He felt the vibrations of the horses before he heard them, their fierce galloping tearing up the earth, as loud as thunder.

Through breaks in the smoke, Roland glimpsed black-cloaked men atop massive black steeds. There were four of them, their boots and gloves black shining leather, swords at their sides, faces hidden behind what looked like strange animal masks: the wolf, the fox, the pig, and the bear. They wore riding clothes and gray woolen jackets. Women cradled wailing children against their breasts, running through town, pursued by the riders, who seemed to be everywhere, crossing paths. A few fat geese and a pig scurried through the mud, terrified, squawking, squealing. The skin-splitting crack of a whip rang out. Someone screamed. A horse stomped through the mud mere inches from Roland, dragging a bound and broken man, rope tied around his ankles. Scared out of his mind, Roland was up and running headlong into the smoke, blacker than ever, all turned around, until he collided with another man, frantic, felt the man's shoulder dig into his solar plexus, spun off face-first into the mud. For a moment, the world went quiet. He was in her arms. Seph. He breathed her in, a rich, mineral smell, remembered the way Seph held him, the two of them drifting off together into blissful sleep. He didn't want to wake up, just wanted to soak up the peace of this moment, the melancholic pain of knowing he would never get enough. And then he heard the solid clang of church bells, suddenly silenced, kept thinking he was going to wake up—that all of this would disappear, a dream within a dream—but when his eyes fluttered open, he saw only a filthy, toothless shit-smeared peasant bent over him. The peasant shook Roland by the shoulder, trying to rouse him, speaking a language Roland did not understand. And then another horse thundered by, its rider wearing a bear mask. There was the flash of a blade, a chunking sound, and the peasant's skull was clipped in two like a cheap special effect. Roland instinctively raised a forearm, not quick enough to deflect the slash of warm blood across his face.

The flames must have finished eating their way through the bones of the church because the whole thing collapsed in on itself in a rushing wave of dust and splintery heat. The heavy bell careened into the dirt below, a ringing thud, pulling down the rest of the tower with it, a tremendous cracking noise like the felling of an ancient tree.

Roland scrambled to his feet, knees bent, keeping low. He saw the rider in the bear mask pivot his horse, which then raised up onto its hind legs, haloed in the setting sun, a magnificent sight as bold and graceful as a statue. For just a moment, their eyes met, and Roland knew that he had been marked. The horse came back down onto all four legs as the rider's voice rose above the screaming, the roar of the fire, the unceasing pounding of horses' hooves. It was a voice as loud and clear as trumpets, the kind of voice that could clear a battlefield, and even though he spoke another language, Roland understood every single word. "Your god has abandoned you," the man said. "There is only one true Lord. Join us in fealty, in worship, or else all shall perish. Those who choose to disobey our call shall cast their souls to the far reaches of eternal night."

Seph's voice once more threaded its way through Roland's mind, an almost indecipherable murmur, somehow describing perfectly what he witnessed. He heard mercy in her voice, sadness. She mourned for him because she had loved him. And this gave him the courage he needed.

He ran, didn't look back, just leapt to his feet and took off running. At any moment he expected the sound of thundering hooves to close in on him, could already feel the sting of the blade biting into the back of his neck, see the world turning over itself as his head separated from his body and fell to the earth. But there was only the sound of his shallow breath, his pulse pounding in his ears, heart hammering in his chest. Who was chickenshit now? He took long strides over the uneven, stony ground, the smoke dissipating. Soon enough he saw the tree line beyond a muddy plot of farmland, a massive stone windmill erected in the distance, a solitary stone tower. And there, just past the mill, over a low, crumbling brick wall, he could burrow into the darkness within the tall trees. He could hide there. He would be safe.

Then he heard him, the man in the bear mask. Roland heard that voice like trumpets. Every muscle in his body tensed; the cold fingers of fear gripped the base of his neck. The man in the bear mask called to the other riders. Their prey was on the loose. The hunt was on.

Roland splashed through the slippery mud, his boots barely able to get traction, feeling suddenly exposed in the open field. He hadn't thought this through. He slid to one knee, got up, kept going, couldn't turn back now. There was nowhere to go, nowhere to hide. They were coming. He'd never make it. The tree line was still too far away. The noise of the horses was everywhere. He'd never be able to outrun them.

Maybe it was a stone hiding deep in the slick and stinking mud or maybe it was a thick root. Whatever it was, Roland came down on it hard, running at full speed, and twisted his ankle. The pain was instant, explosive. He fell forward, bit it—tasted mud, gritty in his mouth—just as the man in the bear mask blew past him on his horse, so close that Roland actually heard his sword slice through the empty air. Another horse followed, then another, both just narrowly avoiding trampling Roland, splashing him with mud. Once more the man in the bear mask pivoted his horse, only this time he was moving too fast, his fellow riders were too close. Two of the horses smacked together, tangled, crying out in surprise. The man in the bear mask's leg was crushed between the two beasts. He roared in agony as the man in the wolf mask was thrown from his saddle, hitting the ground with so much force that his body rolled over several times, arms limp as a rag doll. The fourth horse tried to stop, slid in the mud and rolled over, crushing its rider, his last sound a muffled snap. It was something to behold, such a graceful animal rolling over, rising, the dead rider's oddly bent ankle still stuck in the stirrup.

He knew that she had saved him. At the very last moment, she had saved him.

Limping now, Roland finished crossing the field and made it to the tree line without looking back, knowing that no one followed him. He crashed through the brush, branches and thorns biting into the soft tissue of his hands, scratching at his face and neck. There was no pain, only the thought of survival, the fear that drove him forward, unthinking.

The light faded and the woods darkened. The air was heavy with the smell of vegetation. Roland continued cautiously, lost his footing, and slid down a sudden incline, grabbed hold of a rotting branch, which promptly broke off. He tumbled down the hill, came to rest at the foot of a tall spruce. His body ached in a hundred places, scratches stinging, mud and blood dried and cracking on his face. He couldn't catch his breath, frozen with fear. And so he lay there, terrified, head resting on a tree root. He watched the precipice above him, just waiting for the man in the bear mask to appear. But he didn't. He never did. Shadows fell. Darkness once more swallowed everything whole.

4

The other goats were the first to get sick, seemingly overnight, somehow showing the full range of symptoms that Hecate had exhibited just before she died. Seph acted quickly. She added iodine to their grain, which acted as an anti-inflammatory, breaking up phlegm, and mixed in a live-culture yogurt to reactivate their stomach bacteria. Within a few hours the goats were coughing and sneezing regularly, breathing shallowly, eyes glazed over and distant. It was unlike anything Seph had ever seen before, the severity of it, the way it dismantled an animal's health in just a few short hours. Soon it spread to the chickens, the cows, even the few pigs they kept sequestered in their free-range sanctuary. Weird weeping sores opened on the cows' legs, which Seph patiently cleaned out with cotton balls dipped in hydrogen peroxide. The chickens shed feathers in bloody clumps. The air in the barn stirred, thick with the stench of death, decay.

Black flies typically spent the winter months asleep in the deep crevices of the floorboards, the window sills, wherever the light could not reach. And yet here they were, by the dozens, bravely swarming the tired animals' discolored eyes.

She would have to go to Taras later and ask him to read the stones. His divinations would surely light the way. She needed guidance in trying times, and there was nowhere else to turn.

There was no veterinarian to call, no one to go to for help. And so she resorted to adding electrolyte powders to the animals' drinking water, hoping to flush out their systems. Beyond this there was only the emergency supply of antibiotics, which she had hoped to never use. She had always distrusted packaged medicines, preferring time-honored homeopathic remedies. There was no telling what effect antibiotics might have on the animals' milk. For all she knew, their flesh would turn to poison. She bowed her head and focused her thoughts. The long winter months loomed dark in the back of her mind. She couldn't even begin to think what would happen if they lost even a single cow, but to lose all of them, all of the chickens, the pigs, would make even basic survival impossible. She worried they would lose people to the cities, to the beckoning lights of the outside world, that she would fail in her role as the shepherd of eternal souls. And this she could not tolerate.

The Lord would not tolerate her failure.

He was testing her, as He sometimes did. She had to believe that He had His reasons. And in turn, her belief granted her the strength necessary to meet this challenge head-on. In this case she decided that the ends justified the means.

Exhausted, Seph went to the feed room to put away the supplies and noticed that the solid hinged door—specifically designed to be rodent proof—was cracked open, a sliver of darkness in the pale light. She pushed on the door, which swung slowly open. There stood little Likho within a blade of light, his malformed head tilted slightly to the side, one eye gleaming orange, smirking dumbly.

"Little pest," Seph said. "How did you get in here?" She stepped into the tight room and swept out the black goat with her foot. "Move along. This is no place for you."

Likho bleated, hopped forward a few inches, and then hobbled into the barn, where he disappeared into the shadows. Seph couldn't help but notice the liveliness of his movements; how was it that he was still so healthy? Favored by his youth, perhaps. He was only a few weeks old and already so sure of himself. He'd grown faster, stronger, than most goats his age. It was unnerving—the way he looked at you, always seemed to be studying you, smiling that crooked smile. She turned on her heel to leave, stepped back, and felt something crunch beneath her boot. Reaching out into the dark above her head she soon found the cord for the light. The single bulb lit up cold and bright, swaying slightly. Spilled all along the floor were the antibiotics, chalky white tablets and brown glass vials and paper packages, as far as she could see, crushed and shattered and torn to pieces. She gasped and fell to her knees, trying to salvage what little she could from the dirt, tears burning her eyes.

"Fuck," she said. "No, no, no."

A sliver of glass slid painlessly into the tip of her pointer finger, which she pulled out unthinkingly, nothing more than a reflex. A fat, perfectly round drop of blood formed on her skin, bright red and sticky. She put her finger in her mouth, tasted the blood, and was oddly comforted by this. It was such a familiar taste, so metallic, mineral-rich, this substance that tied her to the earth. She closed her eyes and was instantly calmed. Her body was a part of something so much larger. Her worries were of no consequence. None of this mattered. Breathe in deep and relax. OK. Now, who had done this? Or better yet, why would anyone do this? The lightbulb buzzed above her, insistent. Likho. The thought entered her mind that the little monster was guilty. But that was absurd. He was just an animal. No, it was someone on the compound. Someone had betrayed her, sabotaged her. Someone who wanted to undermine her authority. She would find out who it was. She always found out. And yet, still the thought nagged at her, insistent, the image of the little goat's crooked smile. The stress was getting to her. All she had to do was send Roman into town in the morning. Surely they had enough money left over for more supplies.

It was just a matter of thinking, of perspective, reorienting the way she saw the world. Fear was nothing more than loss of control. And all of this was still within her control. She just had to remain calm and keep her wits about her. She'd always been good at that. This was just a test. She'd always been good with tests, because tests revealed one's true nature, and Seph's true nature was as pure as her soul.

There was nothing to fear because fear was only for the weak.

So she went and she visited Taras in his yurt on the outskirts of the compound, something she did only on rare occasions. He wore his black wrappings, his wide-brimmed witch's hat. He invited her in, said that he had been expecting her. Beautifully dyed colorful sashes draped from the roof poles, at their center a black disc, the yurt's crown. She sat on a pillow at the low round table, crossing her legs, breathing in deeply the rich incense. He served her black tea. Patterned rugs lined the remaining latticework to keep out the cold.

"Welcome to the black house," Taras said, sitting opposite Seph. He placed a cinched felt bag on the table next to a folded handkerchief. "Shall we begin?"

Seph nodded, sipped on her tea. She only ever came to him in his space for his divinations, and only in times of great strife, when she needed greater understanding or clarity. There was no reason for formalities, no reason to pretend otherwise.

Taras unfolded the handkerchief on the table so each of its four corners just touched the edge of the round table. Then he spilled the contents of the felt bag onto the cloth. The runes were carved in small, thumbprint-sized fragments of polished amethyst, and their smooth surfaces gleamed in the candlelight. He closed his eyes and grazed his long, tar-stained fingers over the stones, feeling through them, getting a sense of them.

"Today we will do something slightly different," Taras said, opening his eyes, though he did not look up as he spoke, keeping his eyes on the stones. "It is sometimes too easy to read divinations of the future and see what we hope to see— the kind of future that appeals to us. We allow our fears and our wants to cloud the purity of the vision." One by one he selected six stones, arranging them in the middle of the cloth in the shape of an upside-down cross, in honor to the Lord. "What is more difficult," he continued, "and perhaps more valuable, is to work our way back to the past, to see how things have come to be. Only history contains truth because history can be read. The present is always unclear, shrouded in fog, and the future has not yet happened." He looked up and his dark eyes caught the light of the candle. "Therefore it is the future, the dark cloud of the unknown, which informs the past, and not the other way around."

Taras tapped a single finger on the outcome stone, which, to Seph, looked something like a fish hook. "We shall begin here in the ash after the fire," he said. "You see that the laguz stone was drawn reversed—this is not uncommon. You believe that your current confusion will not come to pass, but rather set firm, something hardened as the walls of a prison. No, *believe* is not the right word—this is what you fear. You fear that somewhere along the way you made the wrong decisions and that these decisions will lead only to disaster, perhaps even madness. You fear that the sickness that currently surrounds you will become all-consuming, that the nourishing flesh has gone rotten, the well has been poisoned. Such fear is rational for a person with such great responsibilities. It means that you struggle with what is right. You are always trying to do the right thing. And because of this you must trust in yourself and in the life energy you have created, for this will be the only thing you can rely on moving forward." He paused for a moment before moving to the next stone. "This is jera, which lies in opposition to the laguz stone. Such a drawing can only mean one thing—that these future events you fear are predicated on the promise of a success earned. In other words, you have made a great sacrifice with your work and you hope to see these efforts realized. More sacrifice may be required of you, of those around you. I cannot tell. Otherwise all may be for naught, little more than mud washed away in the rain. I see you are nodding—this resonates. The concept of sacrifice? So let's explore your reasons for doing so. We turn to the next stone: berkana. Once again the stone is reversed, which symbolizes a loss of control." Taras seemed to think about this before continuing, his brow furrowed. "Something has broken free from natural law, a disturbance, and now a difficult birthing lies ahead of us. I'm not sure how else to say it. Perhaps this refers to the Americans entering your life—that they arrived and they caused havoc." He looked up. "Everything you have worked for is threatened. The security of this place, the souls you steward, all of this has transformed into something you do not recognize." Another pause. Seph saw understanding soften the lines of his face. His eyes gleamed. "This is what you spoke to Max of at the residence, no?"

"Yes," Seph said quietly. "I told him that he threatened to undo all of my work."

"Then his music—"

"The difficult birthing you spoke of, yes."

Taras nodded, once more dropping his gaze to the stones. "You see the gebo stone has been drawn next—the shape of the X, or two paths crossing—which points to the gift of love and partnership. There was a balance in your life that has since been disrupted, as if you have lost a part of yourself or your past, a lover you once cherished."

Grigore. It was like the earth itself opened up beneath her and she plummeted to previously unknown depths. There was nothing in that moment, only unspeakable grief. She hadn't properly let herself grieve for him. Perhaps she never would. The emotions were still hot and twisted inside her, something beyond words. Taras reached out and placed one of his dry, scaly hands on top of hers, wrapped his long fingers around hers like a snake around its prey.

"I know this hurts," he said. "I know you hoped to avoid thinking about those you have lost, but their souls are intertwined with yours. Their light is part of your light. It shines through in your divinations. Open your heart and receive the truth. It is the only way to understand." His hand slid away from hers, retracted like part of an insect, back to his side of the table, fingers stroking through the bristles of his gray beard. For a moment she was convinced that she'd only imagined his hand upon her own. The smell of pitch was everywhere, inescapable and sickening. "And this leads us to the present, which is nothing more than an illusion, malleable and out of focus. As I said before, the future has not yet happened, and the present is merely the past. Your being is no more than a collection of sensory organs, receiving the light, an ember burning bright in the darkness. What you experience here in this moment is—" Taras snapped his fingers "—gone forever. Such is the power of the cleansing fire, the earth's energy, the same energy that ties our souls to the cosmos beyond. Look here, Seph, and see the merkstave stone, or the reverse of thurisaz. Let its energy strip you clean of your confusion, free yourself from yourself and disappear. Open up and look into the eyes of the Lord."

She knew what Taras was going to say before he said it, what all of this was leading to. She had known it all along. The black flies in the barn. The weeping sores. The smell of black death getting stronger.

Taras tapped a single finger on the root stone. It looked like a bolt of lightning. "Sowulo," he said, his voice ringing out like thunder. "This is the rune of extreme strength, an energy that contains the power of a thousand suns. It is the wrath of a god, Seph."

This was what she had known, what she was afraid to admit to herself. But there was no denying it now. The Lord was displeased. And yet how could this be? Her soul was pure. Whatever transgression she had made, she had not meant to betray His trust. So much had happened these last few days, so many unforeseen events, it was difficult to process, and yet Seph did not believe that she had done anything wrong, not truly, not in the confines of her heart.

She left Taras's yurt in a daze, stumbling through the night, somehow finding her way before crawling into her bed still in her clothes. Unable to sleep, she thought of Roland. She thought of the tales she'd heard of those who entered the dungeons of the high castle beneath the moon, those blackened nightscapes, those fables of a fate worse than death, lonely souls lost forever. She thought of Falchik, recalling the sound of his laughter, the smell of his freshly washed skin. How long ago all that was. When they'd found him out in the deep woods, returned from wherever it was he had gone, naked and frozen solid. His skin was blue. And his eyes were hungry and black and soulless as a shark's.

Seph squeezed her eyes shut as hard as she could but still the image haunted her, his frozen body, knowing that his soul had vacated his physical form, sentenced to roam some wholly separate plane of reality for all eternity.

So they did the only thing they could do. They cut him apart and buried the pieces of his body in the woods.

It was what He wanted. She had always done what He asked of her, without hesitation, even when it caused her great pain. But Taras's stones never lied. Somewhere along the way she had made a mistake. Her thoughts turned to Roland once more. If only she knew what he was going through. If only she could somehow understand.

5

Everything was gone. Roland was lost in the darkness once more. He no longer heard Seph's voice, appreciating only in its absence the comfort it had given him.

Trapped there in the black at first there was nothing, but also there was everything. There was the memory of the time he had almost drowned in the Pacific as a boy, caught in a riptide, the rippling white sun dancing, so far away, on the surface of the water. There was the thrill of flooring the gas pedal in his friend's old Charger over the crest of a hill on some backwoods nighttime joyride, high out of his fucking mind on Oxy. There was the first time he'd lost himself inside the body of another—descending to some primal, blood-soaked place—fucking out of pure feeling, without thought, with no awareness of himself at all.

How amazing all of those things had been, each capable of a power beyond words, and yet how little he had cherished them. How much he would give to hoard them once more, experience everything again in all its splendors.

It was almost as if another person had lived his life, wearing his skin, leaving him only with vague impressions of how things had been, how they must have felt. His memories were incomplete. He'd never even been there—anywhere at all. An unbearable jealousy stirred, blotting out his clarity of vision with stains of red.

Nothing had happened.

If his words no longer lived in the memories of those he'd known, he may as well have never said anything at all.

It was all lies, illusions, indecipherable whispers in the dark.

There was the sense of satisfaction he'd felt when his first band had really clicked—playing one of the early Misfits songs, something stupid and easy—when all of the instruments came together, the sloppy chorus soaring. There was magic in that. He'd wanted to play that song, feel that feeling, over and over again for as long as he lived.

But that was another him—another life.

He was losing sense of himself, breaking apart, so far down into his own feelings and thoughts that he'd disappeared, curled into nothingness. Opening up again. He was aware of something raw taking shape, the knowledge of something much larger, that he was just a cell in the blood of the body of a massive being. Because the body was truly the mind's prison. Once there had been a whole world here, spanning space and time, spanning tissue, and Roland could sense the memories of its existence intermingling with his own. That world had long ago been swept clean by fire. What was left behind was nothing more than shadows. The ash that remained swept centuries over black glass, coiled and lingering smoke trapped and cold to the touch. A pantheon hidden in the murk, hallowed halls lined with great stone pillars and scorched by storms of ash and embers. Colossal beasts had lumbered in the dark rifts between this world and the next, their final resting places now the darkest trenches beneath the high seas.

He saw it now unfolding before him, an expanse of utter nothingness.

Across this vast black plane the man in the bear mask made long strides, closing in on his prey. He was master of this realm, wanderer between two worlds, still wearing his riding clothes and his gray coat, black-leather boots and gloves. Once he was close enough Roland saw that the bear mask, which had appeared wooden and grinning from a distance, was in fact textured with real fur, glistening red tissue where the eyes had been roughly snipped out.

"He sees you," the man in the bear mask said. "He believes that you are ready."

Time to give in. There was no other way.

Roland lay back onto the large wooden wheel, naked, straddling the hub with his legs. He stretched both arms above his head. The man in the bear mask fastened Roland's wrists and ankles to the rim of the wheel with leather straps. It was uncomfortable—the radial spokes dug into his spine, the flesh of his back—but Roland did not mind. Anything was better than the corrosion of sheer absence. He wanted to feel something again, to rediscover those fleeting moments of bliss and fear and pain and wonder, to remember what it felt like to be alive.

Looking up, Roland saw the other hunters now standing over him, the men who wore the masks of the wolf, the fox, and the pig. They spoke in low tones to one another in a language he did not understand. And then they were gone.

The man in the bear mask reappeared directly over Roland's head, upside down. He leaned in close. "This is going to hurt," he said. "Do not fear the pain—it will set you free."

The blows rained down all at once, blows to his arms, his legs. He heard his bones breaking an instant before white-hot pain flared through his mind, lit up every sensory receptor in his body all at once. They hit him over and over again, anywhere they could. Roland cried out, begged them to stop. He tried to move his arms and legs, but his body wouldn't respond. It was excruciating—a pain he'd never before known possible—sinews ripping, flesh ragged, tearing on fragments of bone. The solid spokes of the wheel held strong while Roland's limbs shattered and bent and cracked and split open. He could no longer form words of protest, his cries high pitched and horribly desperate. And then it was over. The blows stopped. Roland was left trembling uncontrollably, pulling in shallow breaths, unable to even begin processing the pain.

His entire being radiated a raw, aching agony.

They raised him up into the air, slowly, and with great effort. The wheel had been mounted to a tall post, buried deep in the ground below. Roland's head hung loose, his face slick with sticky warm blood, strands of saliva hanging from his open mouth.

This is what he'd wanted, wasn't it. If only he'd been able to admit it.

He was fated.

There was the time he'd gotten shitfaced at a club before a show and tried to slash the snobby sound engineer with a broken beer bottle. What about that time he'd invaded the home of his childhood friend, knowing his parents were away on a cruise, and taken as much as he could carry. Or the time he'd woken up hungover in the apartment of some woman whose name he didn't even know, some lowly addict passed out next to him, needle still in her arm, and left her there—not even bothering to check if she was alive or dead, her baby in the next room wailing in its crib, its diaper unchanged for who knew how long.

What did that even matter anymore? The distinction seemed trivial.

Dead was dead.

Grigore was dead, and he'd killed him. That's what it meant. Stabbed him in the guts. Felt his blood run over his hands. And it wasn't because he was trying to protect Max. He didn't give a shit about Max.

Be honest with yourself.

He'd done it because he hated Grigore. He'd done it because Grigore was an asshole, and because there was something there with Seph. Fuck it, he'd do it again, given the chance.

He wished that he could do it again.

Blinding sunlight filled the sky, acid white. Roland felt his naked flesh burning. It took nearly all of his strength but he was able to raise his head, look out into the world below. Before him stretched wide the lush, green fields of the Valley of Many Sorrows, and in the distance, atop the crests of rock, he saw what could only be the high walls of Castle Drevylan, as flawless and sturdy as any painted backdrop he'd seen in Hammer films. A pair of black towers had been built into the cliffside, the pinnacle rising over the curtain wall, and the rest obscured by the ramparts. It was like an image from a lovely dream—a fantasy.

Time slowed. The pain came over him in waves, each one more overwhelming than the last. Only the ceaseless activities of the flies kept him from passing out. They crawled into his wounds, stung his face. His eyes grew so swollen that he could no longer open them. His throat dried out. And then the carrion birds found him, heavy black crows with razor beaks. The greedy beasts tore away bits of his flesh, tattered his ears, nose, lips, searching out his fluids. Then they ate away at his eyes, pulled out his thrashing tongue. They pulled away his fingernails, severed the tendons of his arms and legs. There was no body. No more Roland. Left without words to express the unbearable agony he endured, the body Roland dissolved. He was an animal trapped within the confines of its grief, lowing misery. A terrible sucking nothingness. There was so much there was only one pain now, a singular organ stretched like a skin. It was everything, perfectly formed, a perfect black orb that rose into the sky and displaced the sun.

From the black was born the light. Trails of cosmic dust like the lines of an atlas, invisible constellations, shared by those great beings who mapped the universe.

Shadows fell over the valley below. And within this creeping darkness Roland woke once more into the prison of his flesh, once again alone and afraid in the all-encompassing black, the four hunters looking over him, talking amongst themselves in their dead language.

He was still strapped to the wheel, alive and whole, miraculously unbroken—yet his mind was filled with echoes of his pain, that terrible knowledge. And then the blows rained down once more, shattered his bones, broke apart his body. They did this again and again; they raised his destroyed flesh up high above the valley until the flies and the carrion birds ate him alive, until he reawoke strapped to the wheel and was broken down once more.

Sometimes they poured grain alcohol into his open mouth, poured cold liquid fire into his wounds to keep him from passing out. Other times they broke only his legs, let gravity be his torturer, the blood pooling and congealing beneath the sockets of his arms. Still others they raised him high, left to rot beneath the relentless white sun.

And once—this was the most horrible experience of all—they raised him up into the sky strapped to the wheel uninjured. He waited like that for an entire lifetime, with no pain, his only torture the endless cycling of his thoughts.

It was the waiting that caused the pain. And like all lifetimes, this one too came to pass.

After that they killed him a thousand different ways, each more cruel than the last. He was made to retain the intensity of each experience, the very low of it, the very high. Never was he offered relief. He came to truly understand the gulf of silence that lay between joy and sorrow. And this was his knowledge. They killed Roland until he learned to step away from the confines of the body, and then they destroyed the body. He was left only with the nothingness, alone with all of the others who had ever worn his skin, lived his memories. They had done their best to annihilate him, or so it seemed, yet here his immortal soul remained, beaming. The Lord filled him with His light. And in this light he would soon be reborn.

PART FOUR
A GRAND
DECLARATION OF WAR

1

Grigore's corpse was wrapped tight in thin white ribbons and laid to rest within a coffin constructed from pale birch. The coffin remained open, left out in the pristine snow overnight so that his skin would not decay. Sprigs of hemlock smelling of parsnips were laid along his sides. Just before dawn, the coffin was brought inside the residence and placed on the long table in the dining room, beneath the massive iron chandelier, fat candles burning bright. Breads, meats, vegetables, and cheeses were put out on serving trays.

Eating was encouraged as it was a celebration of life, although serving or drinking water was forbidden in the presence of the dead. Rather, a single stone washing bowl filled with dishwater was placed on the table in the event that Grigore's soul would use it to wash away its tears.

In further keeping with tradition, Grigore's arms were crossed over his chest beneath his wrappings, his hands exposed, a silver-bladed dagger clasped in one, and a segment of hemp rope in the other. The dagger, Taras explained, was for protection in the afterlife, and the rope symbolic of the tethers binding his soul to this world. It all seemed hokey to Max, a dumb ritual. There was even a handwoven towel folded neatly at Grigore's feet to collect the tears of those who mourned his passing. Max grazed his fingers over the scabby laceration along the side of his head—still hurt like a bitch. He couldn't imagine that anyone would mourn this asshole. And yet, asshole or not, many of the residents of the compound soon arrived to pay their respects. They shuffled in from the cold, silent and stunned, filled the coffin with dried flowers, muttering weird prayers.

Max kept waiting for Seph to show up and pay her last respects, but she never did. It was always somebody else, anybody else. Maybe she was off doing something more important—or maybe this whole thing was too painful for her. Fuck it. It's not as if he looked forward to seeing her. Their last meeting had been more than a little too weird.

The sky beyond the frosted windows drained pale. Time dragged. Nobody talked. A few people picked at their food, unable to stave off hunger. The air in the dining room was stifling, thick with misery. Max had been on his feet for an entire day, or at least that's what it felt like, doing whatever it was Taras told him needed to be done. Earlier that morning he'd watched them sew Grigore's torso closed, incinerate his internal organs in a coal-burning furnace, then collect his ashes in a brass urn. He was numb to it all—all the death. What did anything matter? The only thing he felt were his boots because they were killing him, an immediate pain, felt his knees because they screamed out his age, the gnawing, bleeding pain in his stomach—nothing else. Dead to the world. And to make things even worse, if that was even possible, the drugs were wearing off. His head was pounding something fierce. What he wouldn't give for a cigarette and a belt of whiskey, to forget everything.

He pushed through the swinging door to the kitchen, a man on a mission. The steel appliances gleamed in the cold, sterile light. He dug through the cabinets for a minute or two, clanging pots and pans, until he found a half-full bottle of cooking sherry. Better than nothing, right? It tasted so salty he could barely choke it down, but that's exactly what he did, choked it down, until it felt like his eyes would explode in his skull.

Sometimes he felt indestructible, like living the life he'd lived should have killed him a hundred times, a thousand times over. And yet here he was, still standing, no mere mortal. Sometimes he believed that his indestructibility was his curse.

He had just a few moments to think idly about how nuts all of this was, how crazy he felt, and then someone gripped his arm hard just above the elbow, hard enough to bruise his skin through his sweatshirt. Max knew that scorched-ear-wax smell; it made his skin crawl. He spun around and stood face to face with Taras, his creepy overlord.

"We agreed you would be on your best behavior," Taras said, as smugly as possible. He nodded at the empty bottle of sherry. "So what's this?"

"Feed me more heroin and I'll be good," Max said. He flashed his best shit-eating grin. God, he was tired, just fucking fed up. "Otherwise I'm not here to work as an usher for your depressing little funeral home."

Taras's fingers dug in tighter, capable of more strength than Max would have imagined possible from such a wiry dude, scary amounts of strength. His hand went dead and the bottle shattered on the tile floor. Black visions unspooled through his mind like tentacles. He saw a giant bat wearing a Stahlhelm spreading its wings over a pulsing medieval battlefield, its eyes glowing red. He saw the skin rot away from a man's face in time-lapse footage, leaving only unblinking eyes—blasted, a screaming skull. And then there was an image of a cliffside castle crumbling into the wine-dark sea, thousands of snakes with human heads raining from the molten sky.

Max came to his senses, ripped his arm free from Taras's grip. The spooky nightmare visions evaporated, instantly forgotten. Blood flowed through his veins again, tingling. His mind was clouded, traces of unpleasantness swirling somewhere just beneath the surface.

"A man lies dead in the next room," Taras said, nearly hissing. "Have some respect."

"Look at this," Max said, pointing at the gash on his head. "That motherfucker pistol-whipped me. He hit me so hard my teeth bit together and I chipped a tooth. Look. He was going to kill me—I saw it in his eyes. And you tell me to *have some respect?*"

Taras glared at him. "He was there to keep you from harming yourself, as I remember it."

Max didn't miss a beat. "That's bullshit. Just like you not telling me where the fuck Roland is."

"So that's what you're so upset about?" Taras smirked. "I've told you already, he is in the custody of the authorities."

The idea of these crazy fuckers handing Roland over to the cops was laughable. Max's confusion found its focus, turned to righteous anger, coursed through his veins. Or maybe it was the cooking sherry. Who the fuck cared? The sheer sensation of it—whatever it was—made him feel sick, his heart pounding, sour sweat breaking out under his arms, over his face.

He didn't want to admit to himself that it felt good to feel sick like this.

It felt normal.

"The police?" he said. "More bullshit."

"I assure you it is not," Taras said. "Though we do not answer to the police, of course—we answer to a higher power.

Now get a broom and sweep up this mess. Do it now. If you choose to disobey any more of my orders, you can plan on going to sleep without your medicine."

Taras turned and left the kitchen, the door swinging behind him.

It took every ounce of his self-control, but Max swallowed his pride and, for the hundredth time that day, did as he was told. Who was he kidding, he had no choice. He knew it. Taras knew it. Seph fucking knew it, wherever the fuck she was. He was a coward. When he was done sweeping, he dumped the dustpan into the garbage and briefly contemplated using one of the shards of glass to slit his wrists. But of course he couldn't do it. He didn't have it in him.

So he returned to the dour gathering in the main room.

An eternity or so later he watched as Roman stood before the coffin in the center of the room, got everyone's attention, and announced that it was time to transport the dead to his final resting place, where he would begin his transformation.

The mourners filed outside into the pale cold like it was something they'd done a hundred times before, as rehearsed as a fire drill. Taras told Max to bundle up, handed him a wretched old overcoat, which reeked of mothballs and dust, its interior lining barely hanging together. But it was warm, and that was all that mattered, because the early morning winds were grim and unforgiving. Wearing this oversized jacket, his head shaved, eyes blacked, he had truly become one of them, another nameless Uncle Fester.

He looked around at the others. It suddenly occurred to him that everyone here was trapped, that they were most likely here because they were fleeing their lives. They were scared, desperate. How many of them had been broken down, stripped of their identities?

How many of them were stuck here like him?

The coffin's lid was sealed in place. Max and three others each got beneath a corner and marched it outside, where they placed it in a wooden sled hitched to a sickly, decrepit horse. Its eyes were glassy, bloodshot. Each breath it took was ragged and wet. Its legs festered with weeping sores. Working this old beast was surely an act of cruelty.

Someone laid a bearskin over the coffin while Taras took the reins, seemingly oblivious to the horse's terrible condition. He leaned forward, said something to the animal in Ukrainian, his voice soothing, encouraging, and the old beast took a few tentative steps, breathing heavier. The sled groaned, its curved wooden skis scraping against the gritty ice.

The sky was overcast, a gleaming monochrome, colder than ever, and Max wasn't wearing any gloves. The cold ate away at him, robbed him of his breath. His eyes teared up in the wind and clumps of ice formed in his eyelashes.

They marched through open fields and entered the decaying expanse of the woods, where all of the sounds changed, went weird. Then they passed beneath a wrought-iron archway and entered an ancient cemetery, its snow-capped headstones tilted, weathered smooth, pushing up through the frozen earth like so many slender gray fingers.

In the center of the cemetery, the many branches of a dead tree were lined with fat crows, quietly bearing witness to the goings-on. The ground was uneven and long blades of dead discolored grass twisted in the wind. Taras mercifully halted the horse, its legs trembling, and grabbed an electric lantern hanging from one of the sled's posts. Under his other arm, he held the brass urn containing Grigore's ashes. Max was once more summoned to serve as pallbearer. He helped carry the coffin beyond the gravestones and up a winding footpath.

They came to a row of tombs built into the sloping hillside. There were three of them, three tombs, and each one was sealed with a barred iron door, flanked on either side by marble columns, and arched with intricately engraved stone. Among the symbols carved into the stone, Max recognized a series of runes, as well as the symbol of the Leviathan cross, something he'd seen on a dozen album covers, now taking on an entirely new dimension of meaning.

Taras directed Max and the others to stand before the nearest tomb and conjured a ring of long keys from one of the many folds of his black robe. He unlocked the iron door, tumblers snapping coldly into place, the entranceway a gaping black maw. The rank smell of fetid earth—soily and thick with rot and ruin—breathed up out of the darkness, made Max's knees go wobbly. He looked back down the footpath and saw that the rest of the procession had hung back in the cemetery, just standing around, watching them from a distance. He noticed that the crows had abdicated their post, couldn't blame them.

"Follow me," Taras said. He switched on the lantern and passed through the archway.

There was just barely enough space for the four of them to squeeze through with the coffin, and even then, it still took some creative maneuvering. Taking up the rear corner, Max had little choice but to blindly follow. He saw little in the darkness. As they marched deeper, the smells of dust and decay grew stronger. It was a stench unlike any other, evil, layered in time.

They entered some sort of cramped, low-ceilinged chamber and placed the coffin onto a stone altar in the center of the room. In the lantern light, Max saw that each of the walls was lined with horizontal alcoves, carved two or three feet deep into the stone. Without warning Taras killed the lantern and darkness swallowed the room. Only a single streak of blue light angled through a crevice in the ceiling, radiant and cool. Mist swirled in the air. It took a moment or two for Max's eyes to adjust, still reeling from the blinding-white ice and snow. Then everything came into focus. In one of the alcoves Max saw the collapsed form of a human skeleton, its yellowed bones heaped in ragged scraps of rotting cloth. A black, putrescent liquid had congealed on the lip of the stone, a fungal muck. He didn't understand what he was looking at. Peering even deeper he saw a pair of tiny glowing eyes blink out, disappear into the darkness, heard the hungry squeaking sounds of rats, everywhere all around him. The little fleabags disgusted him. He recoiled in fear, something crunching beneath his boots, brittle bones perhaps.

And then he realized what this place was, what that black muck was, and what they were planning to do with Grigore's dead body—what they had done with so many others.

"Fuck," he said, covering his mouth with his hand. "Why did you bring me here?"

"Remove the lid from the coffin," Taras said, ignoring Max's question. "We should not spend too much time in here—this is no place for the living."

The other three men, perhaps knowing something that Max did not, moved quickly, barking commands to one another in their language. They disassembled the coffin with their bare hands, the nails squeaking as they slipped free of the birch. Taras removed the lid from the urn and carefully spread the ashes over the corpse, taking time to smooth them into the white bandages. When he was done, the bandages were coated evenly in a black film. He dumped the rest of the ashes on the floor around the altar. Then the others grabbed hold of the body around its ankles, its waist, and shoulders. Only a moment later and they sidestepped Grigore's corpse closer to the wall, inflexible as wood, slid the cloth-bound body into an alcove at knee height, where it tucked away neatly, out of sight.

Taras turned to Max. "You were brought here to bear witness, as penance for your role in the death of one of the Lord's children, to wash clean the blood on your hands. That is what the Lord wanted. That is what you owed. Soon Grigore's soul will move on to the next world, under the watchful gaze of the Lord, to join his blood kin." He paused, studying Max's face, deciphering its shadows. "In this he will be transformed—living in the light. When the stars align with the portal of the astral tomb, the path will be cleared, and the souls that rightfully belong to the Lord will ascend, becoming one with the ever-expanding corpse of the universe, He who lurks in the space between the stars."

"Leviathan," Max said.

Taras nodded slowly. He spoke gently. "You are beginning to understand. Perhaps even to believe." He looked to the other men. "Our work here is done."

The iron door slammed shut. Again beneath the still gray sky, the men made their way down the footpath back to the cemetery, where they joined the others.

Max was surprised to see Seph among them, clad in a long black jacket and combat boots, her hair pulled back in a high ponytail, face severe, lips thin and colorless. She made steely eye contact with Max but said nothing, did nothing at all to acknowledge his presence—just stared right through him like he was a ghost. Who's to say he wasn't? But still, it was impossible to ignore that her eyes were red and puffy, as if she had been crying. Taras approached her and the two of them exchanged a few words out of earshot.

The wind rustled the trees, a sound like flowing water, like the passage of time. Max felt at peace, something he hadn't experienced in quite a while. He truly felt cleansed. The world spun calmly around him, wrapping him in its beautiful web of sounds.

Walking single file behind the creeping horse-drawn sled, the procession once more passed beneath the wrought-iron archway and entered the woods. Suddenly the sky was flooded with the cawing of crows, hundreds of them, streaming black forms flying one way and then another in a delicate, nebulous dance. They settled in the high trees, squawking, riding out the wind, the empty sky gently shifting sideways in rhythmic waves.

Max heard someone up ahead yell out in Ukrainian. A woman gasped. Two men ran off into the woods. There was more yelling. A general sense of confusion seemed to overtake the procession, everyone murmuring, jostling to see what was happening.

What happened next was like something out of a dream.

There was Roland, standing perfectly still at the top of a small foothill, at the base of a large, dead tree. He was fully naked, barefoot, his face partially eaten away from a gnarly case of frostbite. His skin was wind-whipped pink, arms and legs crisscrossed with long red scratches.

Max pushed past the people in front of him, trying to get closer. He couldn't hear what was going on, still too far away, though it was clear that, despite all the commotion, Roland just continued to stare vacantly into the distance, unaffected. As he drew closer, Max saw Seph approaching the scene. She threw the bear skin over Roland's shoulders to warm him.

And then he was there, before Roland, next to Seph.

In that moment, standing barefoot in the freezing cold, wrapped in the heavy fur of that ferocious beast, Max saw that Roland's eyes were as black as a shark's. Perhaps sensing that something was wrong, the crows in the forest loudly flocked to the ever-flowing expanse of sky.

Max turned to Seph, seeking answers. What could this possibly mean? He watched helplessly as she covered her mouth with her hand, her eyes filled with horror. And before he even had a chance to say anything, Taras swooped in and guided Roland down the hill toward the sled, loaded him up. Seph quickly followed. And then they were gone, leaving everyone else behind, the trees whispering through the deafening, chilled wind.

2

Once, when she was a child, Seph asked her mother how big the Lord was. They were somewhere out in the woods beneath the stars, these very same woods, zipped up tight together in a single sleeping bag. She could just barely hear her father's snoring on the other side of the crackling campfire. Seph's mother smiled lovingly. The Lord is so big, she said, that our entire universe fits in the black spot at the center of His eye. But if we are so small, then how does He see us? Seph said. He sees us as nothing more than specks of dust. Seph thought about this for a moment. But if we are just specks of dust then how does He know to love us? He loves us because it's so very cold where He lives, and we keep Him warm, my child, just like the blood that flows through your veins. She took Seph's hand in hers and placed it against her breast. Do you feel that soft pushing? That's the beating of my heart. That's what love is—constant and ever-flowing warmth. We are filled with His love. It's only when you're alone that the cold gets into you and won't let go.

Even in death we remain together, she said, because we are His children. She kissed her daughter on her forehead. You never have to worry about being left alone, my love.

Seph grazed two fingers over the spot of her mother's kiss, as if it were fresh, as if she could still feel her mother's lips on her

182

skin, a swelling in her breast. It's true, she thought, as we get older we come to understand the true meaning of our words.

Like Falchik before him, Roland had been cast out, left to the cold, and it had all come down to her decision. It was something she would have to live with forever. Her decision had broken Roland down and the cold had gotten inside. And now he suffered from the worst case of frostbite Seph had ever seen—the tips of two of his fingers had turned bluish-black, patches on his face, as well as the lobe of one ear, several of his toes—and yet still he did not seem to be in any pain, as if he felt nothing at all. Amputation was not out of the question. Seph eased his feet into a basin of warm water, saw how his skin was already starting to blister, a bruised and angry purple, and studied the strange pink scratches etched all over his body, wondering what could have caused them. Even stranger was the fact that the self-inflicted scars along his chest and upper arms seemed to have faded, if not disappeared completely. After a few moments, she wrapped a thick wool blanket over his shoulders and then sat down, facing him.

There was nothing behind his eyes, only a hollowing, filled with dark space.

Alone with him, down in the bunker and away from prying eyes, she clasped her hands together, leaned forward in her chair with her elbows on her knees. Even though he had been returned to his cell, once more behind bars, Seph left the door wide open. She listened to the steady hum of the air vents. Surely people were starting to talk by now, spreading rumors about the American, the one who returned from his judgment—marked. Later she'd have to think of something to tell them, something to quell their fears, to explain why she'd left them behind to speculate. In the meantime she'd sent Taras back to calm things down.

She couldn't worry about that now. Now, she had her own questions.

"Tell me where you've been," she said.

Roland turned in the direction of her voice. She couldn't bear to look into his eyes, immediately dropping her gaze to her hands, more than a little surprised at how tightly her fingers were intertwined, skin white with tension. Her heart thudded at the base of her throat, anxious, an awful choking sensation.

"I've been to the black lands," he said, his voice flat, void of emotion. "I haven't been anywhere at all. I've been here the whole time, ever since the beginning."

"Tell me what you've seen," she said.

"I've seen the bear, the wolf, the pig, and the fox."

She'd never told him about them, at least not in such detail—the spirits of the forest—the Lord's faithful riders. Seph had grown up hearing tall tales of these men, their acts of bravery in the holy war against the soldiers of Christ. There were four of them just as all things came in four: the four seasons, the four phases of the moon, the four winds, the four cardinal points, and the four elements. Each represented a facet of the Lord's inherent goodness: the bear was the symbol of strength, the wolf loyalty, the pig abundance, and the fox cunning.

"His messengers," she said knowingly. "And what did they tell you?"

"They said that He sees me."

She breathed deep. That wasn't what she expected him to say. She didn't know what she expected him to say—just not that—anything but that.

They were all just specks of dust, weren't they? How could the Lord see him?

"He sees you," she said softly, her voice nothing more than an echo.

Roland's head tilted slightly. "He showed me the black egg of all creation—the solar halo His crown—and then He promised me that I would be reborn in time to melt the ice."

Her heart raced. Was this true? How could this be?

"What do you mean by *melt the ice*?"

Roland said nothing, just stared. Seph decided to move on.

"Tell me more about what happened to you," she said.

And so Roland told her more. He told her about the black chamber in the dungeons beneath the high castle, and the fire that engulfed the medieval church, the ringing thud of the church bell as it crashed into the ground below. He told her about being hunted by the riders, strapped to the breaking wheel, and then he told her about the breaking of his bones, the agony of his broken body, of the razor-sharp beaks of the carrion birds tearing through his skin. He described the dread of feeling his wounds knit closed, all the while knowing that they would once more be torn apart. He described the itching of waiting, what it felt like to suffer through several lifetimes of only waiting and pain.

He described the unending horror of the time he did not die.

She wept for him, for what he had endured, for what Falchik must have endured. Her tears built up steadily as he spoke and then they pushed over her final barrier, whatever was left to hold things in, went wild. She wept because she did not understand what any of this meant. She did not know what she was supposed to do. Everything was out of her control.

Always she had done the right thing—what she believed the Lord would have wanted.

"He forgives you," Roland said, sounding so much different, so much more human, so much like her memory of him. That sweet, sweet man.

"For what?" she said, her voice surprisingly thick, choked

up. "What do I need forgiveness for?"

But he said no more. He'd said enough apparently, once again sitting motionless in his chair, eyes dead, fixed on nothing at all. She grasped at fleeting, frantic thoughts. *The black lands. The spirits of the forest. Church burnings. Breaking wheels. Melting the ice.* None of it made any sense, just bits and pieces of madness, traumatized ramblings.

Seph wiped the tears away from her eyes with the sleeve of her shirt and took a deep breath, steadying herself. Get it together. Stay strong. And then something strange caught her attention—something was different. She fell forward from her chair, on her hands and knees at Roland's feet, crawling. It was impossible. She wrapped her hand around the back of Roland's calf, raised his leg from the water. It was impossible, yet there it was. The purple blistering over the metatarsals of his foot had disappeared, leaving behind only blotches of shined and pink tender skin. She pressed lightly with her thumb, saw the skin go white at first before flushing red with blood—healthy tissue, restored circulation.

She straightened into a kneeling position, inspected Roland's hand, the dead and blackened fingers that, only minutes ago, she believed would need to be amputated. The frostbite was still there, the skin around his knuckles still discolored, but it had lessened noticeably. She stood, took a few steps back, aghast. He was healing. Somehow he was healing himself. That was why his scars had lessened.

The blanket draped over his shoulders had soaked through as his long hair had thawed. Rivulets of water rolled over his broad chest, smearing in the dark hair in the darkened folds of his belly. Roland's face had also regained some of its natural, reddish complexion. She'd never seen anything like this before—had never seen frostbite heal so quickly, so fully.

"Roland," she said. "Are you in any pain now?"

Again he adjusted his head slightly in the direction of her voice. "There is no pain," he said. "There is only the idea of pain. There is only the itching of waiting."

The truth came to her then and she felt so very stupid that it had taken her so long.

She chose her next words carefully, really thought them through.

"This place where you were," she said. "Was it cold there? Or was it warm?"

"It was cold at first," he said. "And then later it was warm."

Everything clicked into place. How could she have been so stupid? Of course it had always been him—it had always been Roland. Max was just a cog in the machine, turning its teeth, important, yes, but ultimately inconsequential. His task had been to bring them the vessel for the Lord's true purpose—this husk of a human being—to deliver His message to the rest of the world. And now that she knew that, Max was no longer needed.

She laughed to herself, couldn't even help it. It was so absurd. All this time and they had never understood. Taras must have misread his stones, all those many months ago. Either that or he was full of shit. But she'd always known. She had. Deep down, she'd always known that Roland was special.

He was the one they had been waiting for.

They had much work to do. Now they could focus entirely on the things that mattered: making music, restoring the health of the animals, getting more supplies for the winter. They'd have to move fast. Too much time had already been lost.

"There is one final question I have for you," she said, surprising herself, surprised that she'd never thought to ask such a question before, dizzy with what the answer might be.

"What is it, exactly, that the Lord wants the unbelievers to know?"

Roland said nothing.

"Please," she said. "Can you tell me?"

He closed his eyes and hummed a melody Seph had never heard before. Except it wasn't really a melody at all, and he wasn't humming. At first, she didn't know what he was doing. He might have been having a stroke, or choking on his tongue. He made a guttural, ugly noise from the base of his throat—nothing but larynx-shredding dissonance. It wasn't just a single noise, but two, a sort of chanting on one level, accompanied by piercing, atonal humming on another. The sounds played off one another, rising and falling in a scale. It was something like overtone singing, something she'd only read about before, but it was horrible. She cupped her hands over her ears and closed her eyes. It felt like her eyes were going to bleed. She saw visions of the end of everything, of the cities of the world buried under hundreds of feet of volcanic ash, of the sun blotted out of the sky—pure beauty—and then everything went black.

3

The next few days drifted over Max like dark clouds. He was inconsolably cold. He kept the space heater cranked to full blast in his concrete shack, only functionally lucid, skin itchy and clammy.

There'd been no word from Seph since she'd left him and the others in the woods. Only Taras ever came around, materializing each morning before sunup to administer Max's medicine, and then again just before sundown. The sound of that evil fucker's fist against his door was better than music, made Max's mouth water like a dog. Otherwise he only got out of bed to piss in a glass jar. His urine was cloudy, dark. It smelled terrible. He was in a bad way—knew that much. Whatever Taras gave him was making him sick, worse than usual. A nasty red sore had broken out between the middle and ring fingers on his right hand, the surrounding skin cracked and itching like crazy. It didn't matter. He only used that hand for strumming and picking. As long as he could hold the pick between his thumb and his first finger he was fine.

His left hand, however, was still functioning perfectly—he never let Taras inject him in that one. When he felt up to it, maybe two or three times a day, he ran those fingers over the strings of the SG, the little ten-watt amp blaring hollowly. He was inspired by his own wasting away, as weird as that was. The depths of his sickness provided new material. Soon enough he'd worked his way through a handful of feverish, frenetic riffs that honestly weren't half bad. They were maybe even pretty good: stuttering and fragile, thick with tension. His style was more stripped down than usual, simpler than it had been in years, almost like he was learning to play all over again. He felt like that greasy-haired kid down in his mom's basement. All the mistakes he'd made since then, all the bridges he'd burned, all the people he'd hurt—all that bullshit just faded away, nothing more than bad memories.

But something was still missing. The music made logical sense, it sounded good, but it lacked meaning, it lacked vision. There was nothing behind it. He just couldn't get there, just wasn't capable. It remained out of reach, lost beyond the swirl of his confusion.

He didn't have anything to say.

Everything was sliding into ruin, everything all around him, within and without. The compound was breaking apart. Seph's little society was dying, people scattering to the wind. They were packing up their shit and leaving. He heard them at all hours, yelling at one another, arguing over stupid shit, petty shit. Sometimes he watched from his window, peeking through the blinds, usually after fights broke out. They argued over food and water. And when they got tired of fighting with one another, they piled into the vans and the trucks and the old school buses. The greasy stink of diesel stained the air.

At first Max thought that someone would come and get him. Surely someone, anyone at all, would come knocking, tell him they were taking him back to the city, get him onto a plane back to the States. Surely the record label would call and ask what was up. Maybe even Seph would show up, tell him he had to leave. But no one ever came besides Taras with his medicine.

It took Max a while to come to terms with this. And it was only when he remembered what Seph had said about Taras communicating with the record label on his behalf, it was only then that Max realized he was never leaving this place. No one was coming for him because nobody was concerned—nobody cared. This indifference signaled his demise. He spent hours at a time imagining the headlines they'd run back home: junkie rock star overdoses while recording comeback album. Back home, no one would even flinch. He'd always been destined to live out headlines like that. He would be a legend. He was ready to accept that.

Wasn't that what he'd always wanted?

Fuck yes it was.

So Max didn't bother protesting when Taras showed up and told him it was time to lay down his tracks. He was ready. After all, it was his destiny.

The outside world was glistening, iced over, and the freezing moon shone brilliantly in the nighttime sky. A generator chugged lethargically in the distance, puttering on fumes by the sound of it. The air was thick with smoke: the horrible smells of charcoal, sulfur, and frying beef. He heard the flames raging before he saw them, turned the corner around the kitchen and saw a large bonfire in one of the fields, casting its hideous glow. It looked like a hell-scape, coal-black embers pulsing beneath indecipherable, crackling shadows, heaps of splintered and broken wood, piles of discarded clothing, God knew what else. The flames were tipped blood red, rolling and popping, and a noxious green color rolled over the kindling like a low poison cloud. He peered into the flames, their hypnotic churn, and discerned the stiff and charred legs of a large animal pointing toward the sky, the cleft of cows' hooves.

"What are you doing?" Max asked. "What are you burning?"

Taras ignored the questions, just kept trudging through the snow.

Max took one last look at the fire, watched its slow burn. The cold air bit into his lungs. He followed after Taras. The two of them threaded their way through the compound. Things were worse than Max had thought. The place was a fucking ghost town—no signs of life at all, everything abandoned. He heard a door clapping in the wind. All of the vehicles were gone, fresh tracks in the snow. All of the lights had been turned off.

"Where is everybody?"

Still no response.

Max's temper suddenly flared. "I have had enough of you ignoring my questions. I'm sick of always chasing after you. After everything that's happened, you still want me to make music for you? Tell me what the fuck is going on."

Taras turned around and gave Max a look that was pure malevolence, his face a mask strained by black rage. For the first time Max actually wondered if Taras might hurt him, but then the features of his face softened, like he knew that he'd lost control, unwittingly revealed his true self. He flashed a crooked grin as if to say *oops*.

It was the moment that changed everything between them. If only it had happened sooner, Max thought, he might not be standing here.

"There is no one here to help you," Taras said calmly. "There is nowhere for you to go. If you enter the woods at night you will be dead before sunrise. If the cold doesn't kill you, our traps surely will."

"You're a monster."

Taras laughed his smoker's laugh. "Monsters are the creations of children. The child becomes frightened, so he gives form to the unknown, the great mythical monster." Taras held his hands near his head, extended both pointer fingers so they looked like horns. Then he shuffled his feet, mimicking an animal lurch. He laughed at himself. "But this is little more than a distraction, this hideous beast that lurks in the darkness. It's all an effort to ignore the true cause of his fear."

"Yeah? And what's that?"

"The darkness itself, of course," Taras said, standing tall. "You want an answer to your question? Fair enough. We are burning the dead. Much of our livestock has fallen ill. Seph has been doing what she can, but she can contain it no longer. The men and women who lived here became frightened. They think all sorts of things. They think it's the black plague and that Roland has brought it back with him. They think he has risen from the dead. That he is haunted by evil spirits. Who knows? Maybe they are correct. I was not able to sufficiently convince them otherwise."

"I saw Roland's eyes," Max said, unwilling—or perhaps unable—to believe that the kid suffered from anything other than frostbite. He had to be OK—Max had seen him standing on his two feet. Still, he wasn't entirely sure he believed that. "He looked fucked up."

"I know you are concerned for him," Taras said, "but there is no need for this. Your friend is stronger than you can possibly imagine." He contemplated this for a moment before deciding that he had nothing more to say. "Now come along. We have much work to do."

A few minutes later, they entered the rehearsal hall.

The lights over the stage were on but the heat was off. Taras made his way over to the darkened bar along the wall and opened the breaker box. The sound of the breakers switching on echoed throughout the room, and then the heaters roared.

Max went to the stage. The black SG was waiting for him

there, next to the drum kit. The Tascam 16-track was all plugged in. The mics on the kit had been set up according to his instructions, the very same set-up he'd used to record his first three albums.

He got to work. First he laid down a basic drum track, which Roland would re-record later. He did it all from memory, a tricky thing he'd always had a talent for, drumming along to the song in his head. He couldn't remember shit in his everyday life, but memorizing whole songs was no sweat. Then he worked on the rhythm sections, going back and layering the tracks again and again until he had the sound he wanted, blurry and dreamlike, but with a harsh edge. The first song was twelve minutes long and it took him the better part of four hours to get the sound of the guitars right. It was important that it didn't sound too perfect. It had to sound raw. Then he dropped in the leads, simple but effective earworms, looping in phases. He didn't bother recording any bass tracks. All he wanted was the hiss of treble. Taras brought bottles of water and a pint of vodka. He brought cigarettes and a lighter. He told Max he could have whatever he wanted, whatever would help him create. Max said he wanted to get high, so Taras injected him in the hole between his fingers. Maybe it was even a speedball. Max's heart raced. Soon the sun was up. He was sweating. He kept on working, hammering it out like a pro. He started remembering things, weird things. They played out like scenes of the apocalypse: a giant bat wearing a Stahlhelm, a screaming skull, some cliffside castle crumbling into the sea. He imagined the whole world going up in flames, the shape of a cow's hooves inverted toward the swirl of fire in the sky. He saw snakes with the heads of men. And then he remembered what the kid had said on the train ride to Budapest, a fucking lifetime ago, almost as if he was listening to Roland's voice in his head, whispers of an astronomical clock, the interstellar dance of the planets. We're all just specks of dust. He channeled all of this into the music and suddenly the larger design of his riffs snapped into place like machinery. He moved onto the next song and then the next as if in a trance. The album itself took form, bubbling up like primordial ooze, the same phrases arriving at the same destination each time, always returning to the flatted fifth, unheard themes emerging from beneath the sound, evolving into something that was truly beautiful—beyond his wildest dreams—otherworldly, like it came from someone else entirely.

He was so immersed in creation that he barely took notice when Taras used his walkie-talkie, the crackle and hiss lost beneath the fuzz of his guitar.

A few moments later the door to the rehearsal hall swung open, a blade of light cascading across the floor. Sitting on one of the amps, hunched over his guitar, Max wiped stinging sweat from his eyes, his trance broken. He muted the strings. Two forms stepped into the room, Seph and Roman—he could tell from the shape of their silhouettes, surrounded by daylight—followed by a third, someone who stood nearly a head taller than both of them.

In movies sometimes the dead rose and returned home to those who loved them. It begged the question: What could be better than to be reunited with someone you've lost? These kinds of stories always struck Max as unbearably sad because he thought that people who harbored hope were pathetic. Hope was poison. People who couldn't let go of something even when it was dead—they were poisoned. And only in the echo of these thoughts did he understand how much he had come to care for Roland, that he'd always hoped the kid was unharmed.

He cared because he knew it was his fault.

Roland shambled into the light, and he was certainly not unharmed. He was something else entirely. He was totally gone. There was no person there at all—only the living dead.

The kid planted one of his boots onto the waist-high stage and stepped up, total control, a commanding feat of strength. He towered over Max, chin on his chest, spider strands of hair obscuring his face. He smelled terrible, like spoiled cabbage, and wore black jeans with no belt, a jean jacket with no undershirt. His chest was zigzagged with weird scars.

Max curled into himself. His stomach hurt.

"How's it going, man?" he said, scared out of his fucking mind.

Roland just stood there, breathing loudly through his nose, in and out. He did not seem to recognize Max at all.

"What did they do to you, man?"

"He's here to do his parts," Seph said, barely giving Max enough time to finish his question. "Your work here is done."

She wore a black leather jacket and combat boots. Behind her stood Roman, shuffling around nervously, black hoodie pulled over his head. Taras hung back by the bar, lurking in shadow. With the lights in his eyes, Max couldn't be sure, but it looked as if Taras was smiling at him, making horns with his fingers again.

"OK," Max said slowly. He turned off the amp, leaned the guitar against it. He didn't know where to go or what to do, his head still wrapped up in the music, under the spell of deep concentration. He was starving. How long had it been since he'd eaten something? There was a half-full water bottle at his feet and he leaned forward to grab it.

As he was doing this, Roland unclipped the mic from its stand and slowly lowered himself to the stage, sitting cross-legged, his back to the room.

Max sat up straight and twisted the top from the water

bottle. Just as he was about to bring it to his lips, he felt a sharp stinging in the side of his neck. His teeth locked in a rictus of pain. Intense heat rushed up his throat. The water bottle tumbled out of his hand, spilling onto the stage. The heat in his throat spread through his chest, tightening. He took desperate, shallow breaths, wrapped his hands around his throat as he slid to the floor, all of the muscles in his body seizing at once—his heart—before mercifully releasing.

He pulled in as much breath as he could, while he could. The flat circles of light above him dimmed, surrounded by the darkness, and the room tilted. Not getting enough oxygen. Max saw Taras slink away into the shadows, syringe in hand.

He stuck me with something, Max thought.

Seph and Roman climbed onto the stage. Their voices were muffled. The room was dark. Max felt like he was underwater, back below the black lake, where he'd gone before. He heard a sound unlike any other sound, something he did not understand, the sound of a snake shedding its skin, of lichens slowly strangling stone. It felt like his head was splitting open, taking in light, and that this light filled him to the point of bursting, an exposed nerve in an open wound twitching like a snake's tongue. The sound intensified. His muscles seized once more, the pain unbelievable, everywhere all at once, his heart about to explode.

And then he was falling through a dust-choked chasm ripped open in the darkness.

In the distance, the beacon of light.

He found himself in a dark room he did not recognize. He could not move his limbs, was having trouble breathing. The room began to form in his mind. Walls slid into place. It was his childhood bedroom. He was inconsolably cold. He'd never gone anywhere, had he? His whole life had been a dream. He was stuck in a dream. As a boy he'd never been able to fall asleep at night, always terrified of the dark, of what monstrosities might be lurking under the bed, beyond his closet door. He suffered a recurring nightmare, the kind of dream that faded upon waking, yet left an unpleasant impression. In this nightmare he saw himself, tucked into his bed, surrounded by a group of witches. And these witches watched over him, unable to tell if he was alive or dead. If he even moved his pinky toe, even a smidge, the witches would descend upon him, gobble him up. So he would try to breathe as slow and steady as possible, paralyzed with fear.

He pissed his bed often back then, dreading the punishment that would arrive with daybreak, the crack of his dad's leather belt, the sting of it across the soft skin on the backs of his legs, burning with shame.

Max opened his eyes. The dark flowed into his skull like a noxious fume, filled his mind with horror. He saw the coven of witches—their faces like stretched animal hides, eye holes punched out, dark mouths agape—leaning over him, waiting to detect movement. He recognized one of them, there in the dark; it was Taras, smiling, and he was hungry. Max opened his mouth to scream but already they were upon him.

4

Roland occasionally witnessed some magnificent colossus crest in the starlight, almost imperceptible—a silvery silhouette in time and space—before it entered a slowly spinning wormhole like an insect sliding down a glistening drain.

He had been gifted the ability to travel beyond the mundane planes of existence, to see in all directions with his mind's eye. Beyond the arc of the black sphere he saw the ringed warp of time itself, the progression of smaller and smaller selves that marked each successive jump in his wondrous ascent. Wildly colored dust plumes yawned across light years. And cast from the beacon at the center of all things in the great black sea: massive beams of trembling energy that shone unbroken from eons past, undiluted.

This was the way things really were, out here in the beyond, not just the way they appeared to be—life, that little poison pill of illusion.

So began his dialogue with the stars. There were billions of them. He listened to what they said, heard their language unfold like so many new dimensions. At first it was overwhelming, the sheer scope of it, the sound of billions of eyes and ears opening and closing in the dark, filling his mind with the knowledge of the universe. But soon he learned to filter out the noise, form black pearls of pure perception. He held one of these pearls in the palm of his hand where it hovered and hummed like a mad scientist's plasma globe, strands of light fanning out like so many tentacles, and at the end of each sentient appendage, an eye opening upon stygian vistas. He saw stars being born and he saw stars collapsing into nonexistence, leaving behind only the violent ruin of black holes. He witnessed alien civilizations rise and fall, complex and fascinating lifeforms—massive networks of consciousness—disappear in an instant, in the blink of an eye, nothing more than clouds of cosmic dust.

The sheer sadness of the Lord's solitary existence was astounding, the unending pain of eternity. It was His voice that Roland heard within the vacuum, His voice alone, whispering such miserable truths. Roland was determined to bring these back with him, these truths, to disseminate their misery into the world like a miasma. In turn he would inflict great pain upon the unseeing. He would cause great suffering, oppress the mindless hordes. This was the Lord's wish—to flood the world with misery, to drive the weak to suicide, the capable to murder, and then to harvest their souls. Only then would he be granted the strength required to dip into the deepest, darkest seas, those even beyond His comprehension, experience the nothingness before the creation of life, of consciousness itself, see the vistas beyond the collapse of all that ever was and all that would ever be.

Who was Roland to disregard such lofty ambitions?

Getting back from such great heights took some getting used to, of course, a harrowing experience at first—almost as if his fleshly prison sucked all surrounding space back into itself, the inward pull of those smaller selves, one after another, until he was jarred back into his body—but he'd quickly learned that no real harm could be done. When he left his body he did so only as energy, free of any physical form, of vulnerability and weakness.

Upon return, there was a rush of interconnected patterns, streams of multicolored light flooding between two humming orbs. This was followed by a terrifying closeness to things, a claustrophobic awareness of the pores in his skin, suffocating, milliseconds that slugged by like hours. And just when it felt like his head was filled to bursting, like the endless loops of pain were pulling his very being apart, the terror would come to pass, nothing more than a bad dream. The familiar angles of the physical world would align. Roland felt the surfaces of the things around him breathe, iridescent, shining in different colors at the same time. Here now he found himself, sitting cross-legged on the stage in the rehearsal hall. He felt the weight of the microphone in his hand, the coldness of the metal against his skin, the padded rings of the earphones pressing against the sides of his head. The thunder of the Lord's voice resounded in his skull. He simply did what he could to match what he heard with his own voice.

It was during one of his earliest out-of-body voyages when Roland learned he could create two sounds at the same time, to give voice to the subtext of his thoughts. He began by pushing air up from his lungs, contracting and flexing the muscles of his larynx, changing the shape of the resonant cavities of his mouth. This produced the hum, and moving his lips changed the tone. But there was no beauty to be found in Roland's thoughts. There was only disconnect—atonality, dissonance. He growled from the base of his throat, spluttering somewhere between the burp of a bullfrog and the strained physical force of vomiting.

There was no need to listen through the tapes Max had recorded, no need to warm up, or to practice. The Lord would guide his way. Roland had faith.

He listened as the mics picked up a sound behind him, muffled, like a body slumping to the floor—no mistaking it. He looked over his shoulder, saw Taras and Roman dragging Max away, his legs twitching in seizure. It was simply something that had to be done. There was no time to waste. Max had served his purpose and now he was useless.

Seph crossed the room and stood facing Roland, watching him. Her face appeared longer than usual, cheeks hollow, lips bloodless. She nodded to him to begin. Roland hit the record button. The tapes rolled and the music began.

None of his lyrics were written down because they could not be written down. He did not know what language he spoke, if it even was a language. Instead the lyrics were imprinted on his mind, impermanent, as if streaming through his skull. The words he choked out were thick with consonants, long chains of twisting, throaty sounds, inclined to passionate wailing stronger and more discomfiting than anything he had ever heard before. Yet he knew exactly how to shape these sounds because the Lord had showed him how, showed him the way, how to speak the truth beneath the sound of the singing. And in doing so he would imprint these words on the minds of his listeners—give them the disease.

This was how they would spread the miasma.

Soon enough he was finished. He pressed the button and the burning red light on the machine went dark. The first part of his task was done.

All that remained were the drum tracks. He listened through the tapes again. The songs Max had written were structurally perfect, surging with raw power, muscular in a second-wave way, with plenty of space for Roland to blast away. He got behind the kit while Seph took over on the Tascam. When he played, he was a man possessed, only requiring a single take for each track. All of the things that had once limited his true potential—fatigue, distraction, boredom—no longer mattered. He matched the rhythms of the engine of ruin. Not so long ago he had wondered how the men who built the Astronomical Clock had set its dial. Now he knew.

There were other systems of keeping time it seemed, beyond comprehension, tracking movements larger than the revolutions of the planets.

When he was finished Seph made a rough mix of the recordings, copied them onto two CD-Rs, one for her and the other for Roman. Then she removed the reels from the recorder and boxed them up, right there on the stage. It was up to the record label to handle the digital conversion and the actual mixing. She went about this task mechanically, saying nothing, ripping the strips of packing tape with her teeth. In bold black marker she wrote, *Angelus Mortis – Extinction Songs*.

Later, Roland allowed Seph to lead him back down to the bunker. He went willingly, entered his cell willingly, waited for her to swing shut the barred door, lock him away for good. He had no further use for his body. Like Max before him, Roland had served his purpose and now he was all used up. This did not bother him.

Soon enough, he thought, the great Lord Leviathan would arrive and swallow everything, the world eater. This would be the last judgment, certainly one thing the Christians had gotten right, maybe the only thing. Thinking of the event still to come, the event to end all events, made Roland smile, imagining the punishment so many surely had in store. It would all come as such a shock. After all, their depictions of eternal damnation were unimaginative at best.

Seph stood there mournfully, hands wrapped around the

bars of the cell door. "How long will it take?" she said. "Before it begins?"

"Only a few weeks," Roland said. "Not long after the album has been distributed. We will need to allow some time for word to spread, but people are always eager to share with one another new methods of self-destruction. The rest will happen swiftly."

Her hands dropped away from the bars and she turned to leave, took a few steps toward the door, thought better of it. She faced him again.

It was obvious that she was nervous. He did not blame her for being nervous because she had not seen what he had seen. She had not seen the world of fire and smoke, the end of everything, the cresting wave of blood that would drown them all.

"When we first brought you back from the woods," she said, "I asked you what the Lord wanted the unbelievers to know. Do you remember?"

"Yes," Roland said.

"Please," she said. "I've given Him everything. I deserve to know."

"It might not be what you want to hear," he said. "Have you considered this?"

Seph seemed to think about this for a moment. She nodded. "I'm ready. Whatever it is—I'm ready for it."

Roland closed his eyes. He listened for the Lord's voice, seeking His approval.

"Only in life eternal has the Lord learned that it is better to never be born at all," Roland said, opening his eyes. "The only choice, once we have been born, is to die as soon as we can, and to take as many with us as possible. Only then can we release Him from His prison."

She seemed unimpressed. He had warned her after all. Sometimes the greatest truths are the most self-evident.

"That's it?" she said.

"Yes," Roland said. "Please give these words time to reveal their true meaning."

She left him then. Alone in the dark, Roland lay down on his back, listened to the rhythm of his breathing. Moments later he felt his soul levitate a foot or so in the air, leave his body behind. This bodiless spirit then tilted forward until it was parallel with the wall, arms crossed over its chest. As it drifted upward through the ceiling and into the sky above, it thought once more—and for the last time—of the Astronomical Clock, such a quaint little mechanism. It set its sights on a particularly inviting dark patch between two dim stars and jumped. From here it jumped once more. This time, it decided, it would go farther than it'd ever gone before, until it couldn't safely find its way back, forever a wanderer.

5

Taras tossed a ragged hunk of raw horse meat onto the floor of the barn and waited for the little black goat to emerge from his hiding spot in the supply closet. He didn't have to wait long. Likho poked his head through the crevice between the door and its jamb, investigating intently with his shiny black nose. He looked half starved, ribcage visible beneath his fur, gnarled legs just skin and bone. The little monster glared suspiciously at Taras with his single eye, tilting his head, then at the chunk of meat, weighing his options. He certainly wasn't stupid, this one. Taras took a step back as if to demonstrate that he posed no threat. Likho shuffled forward slowly, never taking his eye off Taras, head bowed slightly, subservient. Then, in a flash, Likho snatched up the meat and disappeared back into the supply closet.

He fears me, Taras thought. And he knows my scent.

The next day Taras put out two chunks of horse meat, one just outside the door, and the other farther out into the open space of the barn. He moved away, close to the wall, and lit one of his hand-rolled cigarettes. Likho emerged almost immediately, quite confidently this time. He seemed to smirk at Taras as he swallowed whole the first chunk of meat. Then he picked up the second chunk with his teeth and sauntered back into the safety of the shadows. Taras finished his cigarette, stomped out the butt on the floor, and left it behind.

On the third day, Taras smoked his cigarette before he put out the hunks of meat, which were now rotting quite badly. He hoped the odor of the smoke and the rot of the meat would confuse the animal, mask his presence behind the door. It worked. As soon as Likho came out from hiding, Taras grabbed hold of the soft skin on the back of the goat's neck. The kid shrieked, sounding eerily human, almost like a panicked woman. Likho frantically kicked his twisted little legs as Taras stuffed him into an empty potato sack. He cinched the bag tight, and though the goat's hooves were sharp, the burlap held strong.

All in all, the task proved far easier then he'd expected. Perhaps he'd overestimated the intelligence of the creature. He wasn't stupid, no, but he certainly wasn't smart. This was what so many of the world's religions got fundamentally wrong, precisely why the life of an animal was worth less than that of a man, or for that matter, a god. Animals were lowly, wretched things, fit to be slaves. Any living creature that lacked the capacity for reason— not to mention knowledge and belief—was by definition inferior. And as an inferior life form, their deaths meant nothing.

Surely the one true Lord felt the same way, considering the pox He'd brought down upon their farm, the horrendous trail of dead it had left behind. Not to mention the opportunity all of this death provided.

It was no miracle that only little Likho remained untouched, spared from disaster. All things are in accordance with the Lord's design. The little goat's blood was pure; surely it held the power that Taras had been searching for. He simply had to combine the goat's blood with blood that contained an equal and opposite magical property and the disease would be born. The contents of the glass vial he wore on a chain around his neck would do just fine.

There was no turning back now.

Soon after Grigore's entombment, their old horse had given in to the pox. Taras had done the butchering himself, realizing only then, standing there in the silver gleam of the residence's kitchen, his apron stained with blood, how to lure Likho out into the open, slimy chunks of meat sliding between his fingers. Unfortunately, without a horse, Taras would have to make the trek to the old cemetery through the deep snow on foot. The winds were breathtaking and the snowfall relentless, coming down heavy these past few days, burying the world beneath a treacherous blanket of silence. The trip itself was quite difficult, took him half the day. Taras was left with no choice but to adopt an old pair of handcrafted snowshoes once he reached the woods. In the hiking pack strapped to Taras's back, an exhausted Likho bayed quietly, his whimpering barely audible over the whipping winds.

There was a certain purity to be found in the woods in the depths of winter. Someday the whole world would know this purity—once the disease of civilization had been wiped clean. Only then could the planet begin the long process of healing herself.

He unlocked the heavy iron door and entered the tomb, pulled it shut behind him. One could never be too careful. Under no circumstances was he to be disturbed. He breathed deep the smell of eternal life. So many smells disgusted him—soaps, especially—but this smell, the rich odor of decay, the accumulation of whole centuries of rot and grime, filled him with something approaching joy. Such smells served as a reminder that man was weak, born to die.

Taras lighted an oiled rag twisted around a branch. When he reached the astral chamber, he mounted the torch in one of the iron wall sconces. Pleasant shadows danced on the walls. He checked the decomposition of Grigore's corpse. The cold had mostly kept it intact, though it did appear that the rats had torn the wrappings free from the face and eaten away his eyeballs and lips. Dead things always wore such sinister grins.

Taras looked to the jagged crack in the ceiling. The sky was just barely visible through the stone, a light dusting of snowflakes twirling.

He began by forming a circle on the altar with his amethyst rune stones, and within this circle, using a stork's nest as kindling, as well as sprigs of dried hemlock, he lit a small fire. The flames rippled as he gently blew on them, feeding them. Soon he had a bed of embers. He held the open palm of his hand over their glowing heat. It was just about right.

He chanted the words he had been taught all those many years ago, the words that were forbidden from being written down, spoken in the secret tongue of the ancients. As he did this, he went to his things and removed an object wrapped in white cloth, which he let fall crumpled at his feet. He had always admired this particular knife's thin, curved blade, its elegant bone handle. The blade was heavy in his hands, glinted in the torchlight as he turned it over. How he relished its touch, the weight of it, the way it connected him to the days of yore, all those many men who had served before him, tasked only with waiting and watching.

The time had come to release the miasma—the black fog—out into the world. Where it went from there, or what it did, Taras did not know.

From beneath the folds of his black robe he pulled free the glass vial attached to his necklace, its dark contents swishing slightly. He sensed a great negativity in Max's blood.

For more than a thousand years now the flames had illuminated the outer dark, offered the gift of the Lord's warmth.

And tonight they would begin the next phase of His great work. Taras focused his energies, chanting still. He conjured images of a group of black-cloaked figures gathered before the guiding flames, his forebears, faces obscured by hoods, bony hands met in prayer. He meditated on this image, speaking to those who had served before him, summoning their attention.

The torchlight was suddenly vanquished and the bed of embers atop the altar ran blood red, flaring up into high flames. Taras continued to recite the prayer, pulled Likho free from the hiking pack. The goat did not resist; he was too tired, too weak. In one hand Taras held the goat upside down by his hind legs, and in the other hand, brought the edge of knife's blade to the soft skin of Likho's throat.

The little goat seemed to be smiling, his tongue hanging from the side of his crooked mouth, bottom teeth slightly exposed. In the flickering, uneven light, he cast a ghoulish shadow upon the stone walls. Then Likho threw back his head, laughed maniacally.

Taras sliced into the flesh of the goat's neck. A second later the flesh thinly parted, brimming with dark blood, sputtering. Likho's body convulsed as the blood fell to the flames below. Hissing smoke fumed into the chamber. Taras continued chanting. He let the corpse fall to his feet, quickly emptied the vial containing Max's blood onto the flames. The smoke grew thick. It was everywhere, filling the chamber, as if darkness had fallen.

Within the black folds of the smoke Taras saw the flat disc appear, spinning, its amorphous surface rippling with jagged bolts of white light. The smoke swirled around the disc, before being pulled into its dark tunnel, thrashing like the tail of a snake. Taras rose to his feet. The sight of it was like looking into the cone of a tornado. Wind tore through the stone chamber, knocking over piles of bones, kicking up great clouds of dust. Soon the disc grew until it nearly filled the stone chamber, yawning floor to ceiling. Taras held onto the stone altar in the center of the room. His wide-brimmed hat was ripped from his head, spinning off into the depths of the disc. There, deep within the black gulf, he saw rolling gray landscapes, waves upon waves of dust and decomposed matter. He saw the beacon of light—the Lord's eye—beaming directly into his brain.

Smoke as thick as black oil came spewing out into the chamber, swimming with voidspawn, voracious animalcules, those that had originally borne the bubonic plague, tuberculosis, and any number of other horrific diseases. The smoke cycled through the room, flowing over Taras like the torrent of a river, before it was sucked up through the crack in the ceiling, pulled through, the sound of thick fluid swirling down a drain. The spinning disc shuttered shut and disappeared, returning the chamber to stillness.

Taras collapsed to the floor, covered head to toe in charred soot, the sheen of ultrafine dust. Only a few feet away Likho twitched, bleeding out.

The dust ate them both, broke them down until they were nothing at all. Taras felt it happening slowly, until black ichor poured from his ears, his eyes, his mouth. Soon all that remained were his empty robes, the empty glass vial, and the curved knife with the bone handle.

Settling, the words of the ancients echoed through the chamber, giving way only to silence, unseen forms still mouthing their shape, and locked away forever.

6

He was dead. Seph was the one who found him. She was the one who found Max dead. Not that it came as a surprise, and not that there was anyone else around to make the discovery, really. It was down to just her and Roman by then—everyone else was long gone—and Roman could not have cared less. As far as he was concerned, they'd left Max for dead and that was that.

But Seph had to make sure. She needed to see his dead body with her own eyes. It was a matter of tying up loose ends, a matter of closure. And so early that morning she went to Max's cabin, didn't even bother knocking. The door swung open slowly into the stale air. There he was, still in his bed, cold as ice. His passing didn't look like it had been a peaceful one—why, she couldn't imagine—but with all the strange things happening lately she thought it was better not to know. Sometimes it was better not to know. His face was all screwed up, frozen in a horrific scream. Both hands were balled into fists and raised as if he'd been shielding himself from blows. There was no telling how long he'd been gone—couldn't have been for more than half a day, could it?—yet his skin was already starting to rot, ashen, a putrid smell seeping through his pores. It was vile, this smell, like the slow rot of earth. Seph recalled something her mother used to say beneath her breath, an old adage supposedly passed down by believers through the years. What was it again? *Decay soon finds those of impure heart.*

Yes, that was it—more words that only now revealed their true meaning.

She covered the corpse with the bedsheet. It was the least she could do. He deserved that much, though just barely. As she did this, she felt relief wash over her. He was finally gone, Strigoi, the one who had ruined so much, who had threatened so much more. And here she was, still standing. She'd been stronger than him in the end. In the end he'd been nothing more than a man like all the other men—like Grigore, like Falchik.

She'd outlived them all.

As a nonbeliever, Max was not eligible for entombment. Even worse, the ground was frozen solid, making it impossible to dig a hole sufficient for burial. Seph was left with no choice but to leave him there, in his bed.

Later that day she ate her lunch with Roman, who suggested they set Max's corpse on fire to dispose of any evidence. Seph replied that this would be a waste of petrol. They would need every last drop for the tasks ahead. Plus, who gave a shit about evidence? It's not like they were going to be sitting around waiting for the police to show up. Roman grunted in response, unsatisfied, maybe even a little sheepish, though he did not argue her logic, just continued eating his bowl of stewed meat, grimacing with each tough mouthful. She didn't blame him. Taras had prepared the stew shortly before his disappearance. Whatever it was—this broth with its oily skin, this pale, tough-as-leather meat—it smelled foul, tasted just as bad as it smelled. But she ate it all the same. She needed the protein, needed strength. They didn't have much food left, mainly just root vegetables and one last unopened crate of MREs. But much like their dwindling supply of petrol, they'd need those MREs in the days and weeks to come.

"Taras never said anything to you about where he was going?" Seph asked, slurping sour broth from her spoon. She already knew the answer to her question, but still.

"No," Roman said, sounding annoyed. "I told you this. Last time I saw him he was hanging out by the barn. I don't exactly keep tabs on him, you know."

It seemed fitting enough, Taras disappearing into thin air— after all, he had first shown up on the compound out of no-where, uninvited—but it bothered her nonetheless. She had come to rely on his powers of divination, his unquestioning loyalty, his willingness to handle tasks that others found, what was the word, *unbecoming*. She felt that she was at least owed an explanation, especially now, when she needed him most.

"He has a space heater, right?" Roman said, his spoon clattering in his empty dish.

"What?" Seph said, distracted from her thoughts.

"Max. He has a space heater in his cabin, or *had*, I guess. One of the old ones."

"So what?"

Roman's eyes twinkled. "I have an idea."

Together they walked to one of the machine sheds, where Roman collected dozens of oily rags and plastic bags. Then they trudged out to the cinderblock shack.

As soon as he stepped inside, Roman gagged on the crypt-like air, the stink of the corpse. He waved his hand before his nose. "Fucking unbelievable," he said, dragging the rusting, old space heater near the bed. "I can't believe how bad this guy smells. And look at this mess, there's trash all over the place." He dumped out the rags onto the floor, started stuffing them into the plastic bags, closing them up tight. Then he knelt down and carefully tucked the bags beneath and all around the space heater, creating a trail that led to the bed. If the idea was to make Max's death look like an accident, Roman could not have done a worse job, but Seph didn't care. It didn't matter. None of this mattered. She let Roman do what he wanted. When he was finished, he cranked the heat to high and motioned to Seph to get outside.

It didn't take long at all. Soon smoke was pouring out of the cabin. It smelled terrible, like burning plastic, chemical fumes. And as the flames shattered the window glass, the sky turned red, cooled into night.

They watched it burn together. Seph was transfixed, found the sight oddly beautiful.

After enough time had passed, she turned to Roman. "I need to go."

Roman nodded solemnly. "Good luck," he said. "I've got the tapes all packed up and ready to go. I'll be gone by the time you get back."

They hugged, quick and tight. "You're a good soldier, Roman," she said. "And you're a good friend, too. I just want you to know that. I'm glad it's me and you."

"Me too," he said. "I'll see you soon."

They hugged again. This time they held each other a little longer.

Seph left Roman standing there before the flames. She did one last sweep, checked the locks on all of the gates, the barn, and the kitchen, ensuring that the sheds had been emptied properly. The last thing she wanted was to leave something important behind, something she might need. She took one last look at the crumbling barn, recalling fondly those early morning hours spent milking the cows, the goats. It all seemed so long ago now, like memories from somebody else's life, all those nights playing music with Grigore, Falchik, and Roman, ripping through their set-list again and again, waiting for the sun to rise, sharing bottles of vodka, like the world was theirs alone to destroy.

When she was ready she retrieved her pack from her room and set out for the woods. She made good time, reaching the stone outcropping overlooking the valley just as the moon reached its highest point. There she built a fire and set up her tent in case she had to spend the night. When she was finished, she stood near the stone's edge, taking in the boreal view, something she never grew tired of. The black forest beyond the valley swayed imperceptibly beneath the royal-blue sky. Moonlight gave the ice and snow the gloss of polished stone, and a funeral mist hovered over the grave-still valley.

This was her heritage, her birthright, and it filled her with a cold resolve.

Behind her, the fire crackled. Seph went to it, warmed her bones. She did not know how long she would have to wait. An hour passed and the flames began to die out. She tossed on another log, her last one. It was all the firewood she had been able to carry. After this she would have to tough out the cold.

Luckily the man she was waiting for arrived soon thereafter. She heard his steed marching briskly through the deep snow, snorting with effort. And then she saw the black beast enter the campfire's ring of light, its beautiful coat shining, muscles cut by shadow. The rider turned the horse sharply, his leather boots gleaming. The animal marched in place a few steps, tossing its mane from side to side. Seph stood, anxious. She didn't know what to do with herself, how to comport herself. A moment later, and with some effort, the rider dismounted, and tied the reins to a nearby tree. He stood all of five feet tall.

Seph bowed to him. "Thank you for meeting me, my liege."

The man held out his hand, gesturing for Seph to rise. Instead of gloves he wore steel gauntlets, polished, and etched with intricate designs. His long black coat was impressively tailored, appearing heavy. Tightly linked chain mail covered his neck.

There was no denying the family likeness. His black hair was cropped close and formed a widow's peak, which only accentuated the closeness of his small, black eyes. And his cheeks were flushed red, skin smooth and powdery white.

Seph's overall impression was of a child playing dress-up.

"I saw your fire," he said, speaking Ukrainian. "Please, take a seat."

They sat on opposite sides of the flames, Seph on a log, the man on a wide stone. He kept his legs close together, his back perfectly straight, impeccable posture, and stacked one metal hand on top of the other, waiting expectantly.

"I apologize for not sending word ahead of time, my liege," she said, "but I felt it important to tell you in person." She took a deep breath. Her entire life she'd wondered how these next words would sound crossing her lips. "The time has come to go to war."

It was difficult to read his face in the dancing light. When he spoke, his voice was restrained, mannered—but trusting. "How can you be so sure?"

"I've seen the end of everything," Seph said. "I've heard the Lord's voice, speaking through another. I've looked into his eyes and seen the blackness of the beyond, the great nothing that waits for our warmth."

She explained the events of the past few weeks. She told him about the arrangement of the recording contract and the arrival of the Americans. The whole thing had initially been a way to make some quick money, she said. But then Grigore had been murdered on the night of the Solstice and Roland had been banished to the dungeons of the castle, according to law. She had only done what was right. Then she described that morning in the woods when they'd found Roland naked, wandering. And she told him about the blackness of his eyes, the nightmarish visions they'd caused as she looked upon them.

Wind blew through the trees. The man nodded slowly, his eyes on the fire. He seemed to be taking it all in, deep in thought. Finally, he spoke.

"When I was a boy," he said, "my father used to tuck me in at night with stories of the great mouth that would swallow all of creation. 'Vasyl,' he'd say, 'when the time comes you must rise to be a leader. You cannot be afraid. It is in your blood to stand tall. You must be prepared to send countless men to their deaths.'" He chuckled. "All my life I've waited for the return. Yet never once did I believe it would occur under my watch." He laughed again, shook his head. "I didn't think it would feel quite like this."

The horse snorted impatiently, released a great cloud of breath like smoke in the cold air, adjusting its footing in the snow. Its eyes gleamed in the firelight, glowing red—a trick of the light, surely.

"I think I understand," she said. "We believe it will feel one way, knowing what we know. But there's no way to prepare for something like this. Not really."

"Yes," Vasyl said softly, sadness in his voice. "I always thought they'd announce it with trumpets, unfurl great banners, pound on their drums as they marched across the fields, that it would be some grand declaration."

They sat in silence for a few minutes, watching as the fire died down, the remaining log charred and glowing orange.

"Did your father tell you the legend of the boy with the horn?" Seph said.

Vasyl smiled, nodded. "The tale of blackhorn, yes? I know it well. There is a boy, a squire, who attends to a great knight, a general. The general is leading his army to battle in faraway lands. One night, while they camp, scouts come back with reports of a mythical beast wounded in the nearby woods, one of the old gods. The general volunteers his squire to help the scouts put the beast down, butcher it for meat. He believes that by eating the flesh of an old god, his men will inherit untold strength. The boy comes back alone, pale as a ghost. The other men, he says, were killed when the great beast suddenly rose in anger, as if waking from the dead. Yet he does not return empty-handed. Somehow he was able to tear free one of the beast's horns, which is black as onyx. Time passes. The boy fashions the horn into an instrument. Soon the army reaches the battlefield and sets up camp to prepare for combat. The men are nervous. They believe they are outnumbered and that the enemy is fearsome. To help bolster their spirits, the boy plays his horn. Its sound is like nothing the men have ever heard before, invigorating, as if from another world. The next day they are eager to fight. Only their enemy does not meet them on the field of battle. The scouts go on ahead and return with a prisoner in tow, a man who has obviously gone mad. The spaces between his teeth are filled with the flesh of his compatriots. Despite his madness, the man explains that all of his compatriots are dead, that they killed one another and their leaders during the night, feasted on the corpses, as if possessed by demons. The prisoner is put out of his misery when they remove his head. Later, the general returns to camp and calls for his squire. The boy does not come. The general asks around. No one has seen the boy. He has disappeared, and taken the beast's horn with him. And yet, for the rest of the war, which lasts years, the general's armies hear the call of the blackhorn each night before battle, giving them the strength of the old ones, and driving their enemies into the mouth of madness."

"Well told, my liege," Seph said, bowing her head.

"Please, there is no need for that," Vasyl said, waving one of his metal hands in protest. "That story is one of my favorites. A timeless tale."

"I have come to believe that the tale of the blackhorn is no legend," Seph said. "As a matter of fact, it is prophecy."

She told him about the album they had recorded with the Americans, about how Roland had seemed to channel the voice of the Lord Himself with his vocals, how she believed that the music they had created was much like the sounds produced by the horn of the beast. Even as they spoke, these sounds were making their way out into the world, where others would hear them, hear their call.

"Every great army must find its strength somewhere," Seph said.

"We can only hope that its intended effect is successful," Vasyl said.

"I believe that it will be."

"I was wrong earlier to hope for trumpets. Perhaps the sound I should listen for is something else entirely." Vasyl stood. "You have been a good shepherd all these years, Seph, much like your mother before you, her mother before her. I am forever indebted to you for your service. Now, if you'll excuse me, I must tell the others what you have told me."

Vasyl climbed back onto his steed, disappeared beyond the light of the campfire. Seph listened as the sounds of the horse faded in the distance. Then she listened to the sounds of the night until the cold forced her to get up and move.

She arrived back at the compound at the crack of dawn,

freezing, utterly exhausted. Roman was gone, as expected. She was all alone. The buildings looked smaller than she remembered, shoddier. Everything was different somehow. The long icicles along the barn roof's eave looked like so many monstrous teeth, golden, reflecting the early morning sunlight. She had really let things go these past few months, let the decay set in.

So be it, she thought. We owe our lives to the dead. It is they who fertilize the soil, who grow our forests tall and strong. It is the dead who fortify the strength of our souls. The body grows weak and dies. The soul lives forever.

After reviewing her checklist twice, Seph pulled shut the hatch of the bunker, sealed herself in her room. There she waited until enough time had passed.

And when she returned to the surface, she undid the lock on the largest of the storage sheds, raised the folding steel door. The engine of Grigore's black 4x4 roared to life as the familiar sounds of Bathory's *Blood Fire Death* tore through the speakers. Seph smiled. It seemed so fitting that the last album Grigore had listened to was the one that had brought Wisdom together in the first place, the one they had first bonded over together, that had sounded like nothing else at the time. They had spent months listening to it again and again and again, dreaming one day of starting a band of their own.

Once she hit the open road, Seph ejected the Bathory disc, cracked open the window, and tossed it to the wind. She put in one of the CD-Rs she'd made of *Extinction Songs*. From somewhere far away she heard the deep sound of the blackhorn, bellowing like the lamentations of some ancient, lumbering beast. She felt the strength flow through her veins, and let the visions of eternal night carry her away.

PART FIVE
TELOS

KIEV, 12:30 PM

S eph drove the 4x4 across the long bridge over the frozen Desna River and into the Dniprovskyi District on
the eastern side of the city. The drab, yellowish buildings
looked washed out against the motionless gray sky. In the distance she saw clearly the gold domes of St. Michael's cathedral
and bell tower. Despite the cold, many people were out on the
streets, wrapped up in their meaningless lives. Seph eyed them
as she drove by. These were the same people that allowed their
children to learn Russian in school.

On the radio, she half listened to a news broadcast about a
mysterious illness spreading through Eastern Europe and Rus-
sia, symptoms similar to the bubonic plague. Seph turned off
the radio. She needed to keep her head straight.

Roman waited for her at the nearest bus terminal. He was
dressed all in black—heavy boots and combat jacket—and
waved at her as she approached, smiling wide. He tossed his
heavy black duffel bag into the back seat, where it landed with
a metallic thud. They drove around aimlessly for a few minutes, catching up. Seph told Roman about how things had
gone with Vasyl, about how she had passed the time alone
down in the bunker, how it had felt to leave the compound
behind for good. There wasn't much to say, really. Then it was
Roman's turn. He was bursting with news, talked a million

miles per minute.

The label had quickly released the album without doing any promotion, took the whole metal world by surprise. It immediately earned rave reviews. The hype was instant. Tracks were streaming all over the Internet. The vinyl copies that were pressed had all been shipped, sold out overnight. Online message boards were going crazy over this thing. There were rumors that the music contained hidden messages, that there was no lyric sheet because the songs were actually occult tenets, instructions for black-magic rituals, invocations, formulas to commune with the dead. They said that Max had disappeared, that he killed himself in order to transpose his soul into the music. These rumors made the album even more popular. Then some kid in America shot up his school and the police found transcriptions of the lyrics in his notebook. That was what really did it. Suddenly it was all over the news. The conservative politicians went nuts, drummed up more publicity than anyone thought possible. Then a singer in an up-and-coming band committed suicide on stage at a festival while wearing an Angelus T-shirt. Some kid cut his mother's head off with a sword and ate part of her brain. People started burning down churches. The first one was in South America— the San Francisco Church in Chile. Then it happened in Norway, in Australia, in the States, in the UK, in Mexico.

Seph couldn't believe that so much had happened so fast. It made her head spin. She wanted to hear more but there wasn't time. She had to focus.

They crossed back over the river and entered the Pecherskyi District, where the Verkhovna Rada was located. Seph circled the fancy government neighborhoods a few times, scoping things out. These people were the worst—these were the ones who sold out their own country to make a quick buck. On the second pass they decided they would start with the restaurant serving Russian food, the one with the large plate-glass window. It was the tail end of the lunch-hour rush and the place was packed with men and women in fancy work clothes, tailored suits and form-fitting dresses. The men wore gold watches, the women gold jewelry. Roman climbed into the back seat and unzipped his duffel bag. They made eye contact in the rearview mirror. Roman nodded. This was it. He was ready. On the third pass Seph floored it, hopped the curb with the 4x4's front left tire, and smashed through the restaurant's plate-glass window, crunching the group of tables nearby, and pinning a man against the wall.

Stunned, Seph grabbed the sawed-off shotgun from under her seat, tried to open the driver's side door, but it was jammed shut, pinned against something. Everyone in the restaurant was screaming. The air was filled with choking dust. There were people everywhere, tables overturned, lights flickering. Then Roman was out on his feet and he was firing his AK-47, bursts of controlled fire. The noise was deafening. Seph still couldn't get her door open. Her hands were shaking bad. She might have hit her head on the windshield. Roman was cutting people down. They were running scared, trying to hide, to get away. Seph saw some guy's head explode. There was blood everywhere. The screaming started dying down. There was nowhere for all the sound to escape to. It was so loud. It was so still. And then Roman was back in his seat, slamming his door shut, screaming for Seph to drive.

Her instincts kicked in. She threw the transmission into reverse and floored it. The guy pinned against the wall fell below the 4x4's bumper, sliding off the slightly creased hood and disappearing from sight. Bits of plaster and glass fell from the 4x4 as they rolled out. Then their rear bumper smashed into a parked car in the street. Alarms were going off up and down the street. Seph threw it into drive. They bolted through the narrow streets, swiping a few parked cars, sparks flying. The only sound Seph heard was the ringing in her ears. She tasted acid in her mouth. Her heart was pounding.

Again she saw the golden domes of St. Michael's in the distance. She took a few more turns, not knowing where she was going. Roman was laughing his head off. There were sirens in the distance, closing in—a whole swarm of them.

Seph panicked, shouting that they needed to ditch the 4x4. She swung the wheel and turned abruptly into a parking garage. From the back seat Roman handed her an MP7 and her AK-47. She looped the straps over her shoulders like bandoliers. Two handguns were already strapped to her thighs. She had a knife in each boot, an ammo pack at her waist that held a dozen magazines. She wore body armor, pads on her knees and elbows, gloves. They both put on their balaclavas and their goggles. Roman was jacked. Seph had never felt so alive. She grabbed Roman's hand and they squeezed tight. This is what it was like to really share something with somebody. This is what it felt like to really believe in something. They got out and started running, their boots slapping against the pavement. They gunned down anyone unlucky enough to cross their path.

The sirens were closer now, louder. And there were more of them. Seph pointed out what appeared to be an abandoned construction site, a deep concrete foundation filled with rows of thick concrete columns, high walls. A skeleton of steel reinforcement beams and wire mesh had been built several stories high.

They climbed the chain-link fence and split up as they entered the construction site. A few minutes later and there were police cars everywhere with their flashing blue lights. Someone called out over a megaphone, telling them to come out, to surrender.

The only way she was going out was in an act of aggression.

For a while nothing happened. It was really cold. The police threw in silver canisters of tear gas, set off flash grenades. And then they rushed in.

Seph focused on her breathing. She used the pillars to slice the pie, only claiming amounts of ground that she knew were safe. She got a couple of the officers, took them out. Her footwork was better than theirs. She was better trained, had better weapons—and she wasn't afraid to die. Then she saw Roman's boots sticking out around the corner of a wall, blood pooled on the ground. They'd got him.

She was devastated—shocked even.

She made a mistake, wasn't thinking straight. Distracted by her grief for her friend. She went for higher ground, climbing the metal steps that twisted around the steel beams. Sparks flew as their bullets landed all around her. She turned and unloaded an entire magazine with the MP7. She screamed into the sound of her gunfire, baring her teeth like an animal.

It was like something punched her in the side of the head. The sound of wind was everywhere—maybe even the deep bellowing of the blackhorn.

She lost her footing and fell over the staircase railing. The last thing she saw was the world turning over itself and the last thing she felt was her bones as they cracked against the pavement below.

ABOUT THE AUTHOR

David Peak is the author of *Eyes in the Dust* (Dunhams Manor, 2016), *The Spectacle of the Void* (Schism, 2014), and *The River Through the Trees* (Blood Bound Books, 2013). His writing has been published in *Denver Quarterly*, the *Collagist*, *Electric Literature*, *3:AM*, and *Black Sun Lit*, among others. He lives in Chicago.

CPSIA information can be obtained
at www.ICGtesting.com
Printed in the USA
BVHW07s0043170518
516408BV00010B/852/P